Here's what teens are saying about Bluford High:

"I love the Bluford series because I can relate to the stories and the characters. They are just like real life. Ever since I read the first one, I've been hooked."
—*Jolene P.*

"All the Bluford books are great. There wasn't one that I didn't like, and I read them all—twice!"
—*Sequoyah D.*

"I found it very easy to lose myself in these books. They kept my interest from beginning to end and were always realistic. The characters are vivid, and the endings left me in eager anticipation of the next book."
—*Keziah J.*

"As soon as I finished one book, I couldn't wait to start the next one. No books have ever made me do that before."
—*Terrance W.*

"Each Bluford book gives you a story that could happen to anyone. The details make you feel like you are inside the books. The storylines are amazing and realistic. I loved them all."
—*Elpiclio B.*

"Man! These books are amazing!"
—*Dominique J.*

BLUFORD HIGH

Lost and Found

A Matter of Trust

Secrets in the Shadows

Someone to Love Me

The Bully

Payback

Until We Meet Again

Blood Is Thicker

Brothers in Arms

Summer of Secrets

The Fallen

Shattered

Search for Safety

No Way Out

Schooled

Breaking Point

The Test

Pretty Ugly

The Fallen

PAUL LANGAN

Series Editor: Paul Langan

SCHOLASTIC INC.
New York Toronto London Auckland
Sydney Mexico City New Delhi Hong Kong

ISBN 978-0-545-45019-5

12 11 10 9 8 7 6 5 4 3 2 1   12 13 14 15 16 17/0

Printed in the U.S.A.   23

First Scholastic printing, January 2012

Chapter 1

"Martin, do you have anything to say for yourself?" Mr. Gates says to me. I can hear anger in his voice.

He's the superintendent of Bluford High School—a large silver-haired man in his late 60s. His lips are pencil-thin, and there are bags under his eyes. Bags from listening to stories like mine.

I know he's going to throw me out of Bluford. I can't blame him. All he knows about me is what he's read in the thick folder on his desk.

I can see the pink suspension notices from my seat. He flips through them like he's leafing through an old phone book. I know the words he's reading. I remember the last letter the school district sent to my mother.

MARTIN LUNA has on multiple occasions displayed severe behavioral problems in school and on school grounds. He has repeatedly engaged in threatening and hostile confrontations with other students, and he has violated school attendance policies numerous times. Furthermore, given his most recent outburst, it is the opinion of this district that he poses a threat to students and faculty. As a result, the district recommends that MARTIN LUNA be expelled from Bluford High School.

My mother cried when she got the letter. I found it laying on our kitchen counter stained with teardrops that made the ink bleed. I crumpled it up right then, but it didn't matter. The damage was done.

Today's my hearing—my last chance.

"Well?" he says. He's looking at me now. He doesn't even blink.

The auditorium is quiet except for someone coughing as I stand to answer him. I hear my mother sniffle behind me. *I'm so sorry for everything, Ma,* I want to say. I feel guilt clawing at my chest like invisible hands.

"Please don't do this," my mother yells out. "He's a good boy. *Please!*" I turn to see her standing at her seat, holding her hands as if she's praying to him. Her nose is running and her voice is trembling. It reminds me of how she was three months ago, the day my little brother died. I close my eyes to push the memories back, but it doesn't work.

"Ms. Luna," Mr. Gates cuts in. "I understand this is difficult for you, but we've already heard what you had to say. Now *please* let your son speak."

My mother sits down, crosses herself, and quietly wipes her eyes. She's never backed down from anything, but this time I know she expects the worst. So do I.

Mr. Gates turns back to me. He closes my folder, drops his pen, and rubs his forehead like he's got a bad headache. I am in trouble. No question about it.

"Mr. Luna, in just two weeks at Bluford High School, you have been in several serious fights. You have cut school, skipped classes, and last Friday in the middle of yet another fight, you struck a teacher. This behavior is unacceptable. Unless there are some extenuating

3

circumstances, I'm afraid we have no choice but to expel you. Now, this hearing is your opportunity to tell your side of the story. Martin, what do you have to say for yourself?"

I look up at him because some of his words escape me. *Extenuating circumstances*? I don't know what they are. But I do know there are reasons why I shoved old Mr. Dooling into a wall, why me and Steve Morris keep fighting, why my anger sometimes explodes like a gunshot.

I never meant for any of it to happen. I know I screwed up, especially when I pushed the teacher. But everything else I did was the best I could do, was the only choice I really had.

There's no way Mr. Gates will ever understand this. His eyes tell me what he thinks—expelling me is the right thing to do. There's no changing his mind. I can see that.

Still, like Vicky said, I gotta try. I take a deep breath and begin telling him the truth, how it started days ago when I stumbled into Bluford a bloody mess . . .

"Oh my God, Martin," Vicky said as she looked at the cut over my eye. Her

4

mouth was wide open, and her hands covered her cheeks. "Who did this to you? Was it Steve?"

I shook my head no. I wished she didn't have to see me this way. I could taste blood in my mouth and knew some was on my face. She deserved to know what happened, but I had no time to explain. Frankie and the rest of my crew were on the road, and someone was about to get hurt. I had to do something. Now.

"I'm fine, Vicky. I'll catch up with you later," I said, but my voice cracked into a nasty whisper. I was dizzy. Too many punches to my head.

"Quick, Martin, inside right now," barked Ms. Spencer, our principal. She led me past Vicky straight to the front office. "The rest of you get back to class. There is nothing to see here."

It was almost time for first lunch period, and a small crowd of students had gathered at the front of the school to see my entrance. They looked at me as if I had just shot someone. *What are you starin' at?* I felt like saying, but I had more important things to worry about.

"Ms. Spencer, I need to speak with someone I know. He's a cop. His name is Nelson Ramirez. I need to speak with him. *Now*," I said. She studied my face carefully, not sure whether to trust me.

I couldn't blame her. Where I come from, you don't talk to cops, and you don't expect them to solve problems. I learned that when Huero, my little brother, was killed. For months, my mother and I waited for the police to do something. All we got from them was an apology and some excuses about workload and too many cases.

But Ramirez was different. He was Chicano like us, a friend of my mom's who grew up in the barrio. He held my mom at my brother's funeral and understood that the day Huero died, part of me died too. Where else could I turn?

"I already called the police, Martin." Ms. Spencer said as I collapsed into the squeaky chair in her office. "I called your mother, too. She's on her way," she added.

My headache was getting worse. The last thing I wanted was my mom to see me this way. But I didn't have time to worry about it.

"Call Ramirez," I repeated, rubbing my swollen jaw. "Here's his phone number. Tell him Martin Luna is looking for him." I handed her the crumpled piece of paper he'd given me over the summer.

"Why him?" Ms. Spencer asked, studying the scrap like it was a fake ID card or something. "If you did something wrong, now is the time to tell me so you won't get in any worse trouble."

I wanted to curse her out right there. Behind her wire-rimmed glasses, she couldn't see nothin'. I wasn't afraid of any punishment she could give me. A suspension? A letter? That ain't nothin' compared to watching your brother die in your arms, seeing his blood drip onto your shoes, feeling his skin turn cool in your hands. And now more blood was about to spill.

"There ain't no worse trouble!" I growled, tired of talking to her. I jumped up and reached for her office phone. But my legs were weak, and the room suddenly felt like waves were rolling through the floor. I leaned against the wall to stop from falling.

"*Martin!*" Ms. Spencer yelled, grabbing me and easing me back into the chair. Her eyes were wide with worry.

"*Please*, Ms. Spencer," I said, pointing to the phone.

"Okay, okay. I'm calling him right

now. Just sit down and don't move," she said, nervously dialing the numbers. "But if there is something I can do to protect you and the other students in this school, you need to let me know."

Protect me? Too late for that, I wanted to say. The room was spinning. I grabbed the chair to steady myself. "Just call him."

I knew it would come down to this. I knew it the second I agreed to meet my homeboys in the parking lot outside Bluford. Our crew—Frankie, Chago, Junie, and Jesus—were about to do something we had talked about since Huero died. We were going to get revenge.

After months of searching, we found out who shot my brother—a punk named Hector Maldenado. We'd talked about what we'd do all summer. For a while, I dreamed about it night and day. It was the only thing that pushed the hurt away. The only reason I had to get up in the morning.

Don't get me wrong, I ain't a gang-banger. I've stolen a few things and gotten into some fights, but I never did something serious like this before. But everything changed when Huero died. I snapped like an old rubber band.

Frankie Pacheco knew this. He was the oldest and toughest in our crew. He got us guns and showed us what we needed to know. And for a while I was ready to let it all go down like that.

Pop! Pop! Pop!

Just three shots. A blast of sour gun smoke. The screeching of tires as Frankie's old LeMans pulled away. The same sounds I heard the afternoon Huero died. That would be the end of it.

But I couldn't do it.

In my head, I kept seeing my brother's face, Vicky's eyes, my mom's tears. And I kept hearing something my English teacher, Mr. Mitchell, said. *You could have a bright future ahead of you. Don't throw it away.*

Call me soft. I don't care. You're not the one who sits at your brother's grave, listens to your mother crying in the dark, and knows what it's like to lose someone. If you were, you'd understand why I couldn't be like the coward who drove down our street and stole my brother's life with a gunshot.

"Yes, this message is for Officer Ramirez," Ms. Spencer said. "This is the principal at Bluford High School. I have

Martin Luna here in my office. He seems to have been involved in an altercation and wishes to speak with you. He says it's important."

I put my head in my hands. A message! Where was he? It was the one time I needed to reach him, and he wasn't there.

Call me anytime, he had said when he gave me the number. Yeah, right.

I felt Ms. Spencer watching me. I knew she was wishing I never transferred into her school. But if I'd stayed at Zamora High, I'd be in jail or dead already.

That's why my mom moved out of our old neighborhood, making me start my sophomore year at Bluford High. I was so angry when she told me, I almost punched her. Can you believe that? I hate when I get that way, but Huero's death did that to me.

The move added 45 minutes to her bus ride to Wal-Mart where she worked as a cashier with Nilsa, Frankie's older sister. But she did it—to *save* me. It didn't work.

"Where is he?" a man yelled into the office, shattering my thoughts. "Where's Martin?"

I looked up to see Mr. Mitchell. The

throbbing in my skull was worsening by the minute, and the room was fuzzy, like an old TV that isn't tuned in right.

"What happened?" he asked, shaking his head. The other day, he gave me an "A" for an essay I wrote about Huero. I wondered what he'd say if he knew another kid was about to die because I was too scared to talk.

I stared at him, my heart pounding. My hands sweating. The room seemed to spin. Overhead, the bell sounded, announcing the beginning of first lunch period. Time was running out like blood from a cut.

"Martin, what is it?"

I knew it would take Frankie at least a half hour to get to Hector's house. It hadn't been that long since we fought. If I acted now, there still was a chance I could do something. But I wasn't ready to rat out my boys. I ain't a snitch.

Up until a month ago, Frankie and I were like brothers. *Family*, he called me and the rest of our crew. I even took a beating to earn that word. That's how we did things.

But then Frankie admitted that the bullet that killed my brother was proba-bly aimed at him. I don't know why I never thought of it before, but it made sense. Frankie was the one with the knife wound, the homie most feared on our block, the tattoo-covered 19-year-old who had enemies everywhere. Of course the bullet was meant for him, not an eight-year-old boy. Not Huero.

The news changed me. It was like I'd been asleep and suddenly woke up. Questions kept popping in my head in the middle of the night, cutting our friendship like a knife. Making me secretly hate him. Why did Huero have to pay for what Frankie did? And why was Frankie free to cruise the 'hood while my brother's lying in the ground?

Frankie wasn't stupid. He knew I was changing. That's why he wanted me to do the shooting this morning. It would make me as guilty as him, and it would mean he'd always have something on me in case I gave him trouble. I'm sure he planned it this way. But he didn't plan on me backing out.

"I'm not doin' it, Frankie. I'm serious," I announced while we were all sitting in his LeMans ready to get Hector. The car got as quiet as a grave.

You should have seen Frankie's face. If it were a gun, I'd be dead right now. I jumped out before anyone could stop me.

Chago, my best friend from back in the day, tried to change my mind. He was worried about what Frankie would do next.

"C'mon, Martin. We're family, man. Brothers," Chago said. "Let's go."

The word stung me. *Family*. It was like a slap in my face. Look what the word did to me—it cost me my brother and was about to turn me into a criminal. That ain't what family is supposed to be. Anyone who says so needs to get their head examined.

"My brother was Huero, Chago," I said. "And he's dead because of something Frankie did. You know it's true. What we are about to do, it ain't family, Chago. It's crazy."

Frankie lost it. His jaw tightened up, and he got this cold look I saw once before when he jumped a kid for talking to his girlfriend. The guy was already on the ground when Frankie's foot smashed into his face with a heavy wet thud. I can still hear the sound. The guy moaned and threw up, and Frankie backed away, acting like he was trying to protect his new steel-tipped boots from the mess. Like they were more important than another person.

Frankie was ready to do worse to me when he stepped out of his car. Don't get me wrong. I can handle myself in a fight. But I'm no match for Frankie. His fists pounded into my face and side, knocking me to my knees. That's when he pulled out his gun.

"You can't leave your family, Martin," he said. His nine millimeter was pointed at my face. It was the first time I looked into the barrel of a gun.

All I could think about was the bloody mess I'd be when my mother found me, how she'd cry at my funeral with no sons at her side.

"I can't go no further. Do what you gotta do," I said. I whispered a prayer just in case.

Frankie blinked.

Maybe it was the guilt he had for Huero's death. Maybe it was that he didn't want to shoot me in daylight where a crowd of people could witness it. Or maybe it was because he was shocked that I was willing to die to prove I ain't a killer. I don't know what it was, but Frankie let me go.

"This ain't done," he growled and

jumped back into his car.

I believe him.

The clock over Ms. Spencer's desk said 10:38. Frankie and the boys had been on the road for 20 minutes already. There were at least two guns in the car, and the only one who knew their plan was me. I was wasting time.

"C'mon, Martin. It's like I said before. You have a choice. You can end this right now," Mr. Mitchell said, staring at me like I was a puzzle. "We're listening."

I could feel myself zoning out, like there was a fog settling over my brain. All last night, I replayed how this day would go down. When I grabbed my bandana and left to meet Frankie, I knew I had to walk away, that Frankie was gonna come at me like never before. But I figured if I could just escape and get to Bluford, it would all be over.

I was wrong.

Looking at Ms. Spencer's tight jaw and Mr. Mitchell's wide eyes, I knew it was just beginning.

Chapter 2

"He's in the principal's office, Ms. Luna. He's been hit in the head, and he's a little out of it. We have an ambulance coming to take him to the hospital," I heard Ms. Bader, the school secretary, say in the distance.

Instantly, the pounding in my head got worse.

I closed my eyes and listened as the familiar jingle of my mom's keys grew louder. Then I heard another sound. My mom gasping.

"Oh, Jesus, no!" she cried, darting across the office to me.

"I'm okay, Ma. It looks worse than it is," I said, shocked at who followed her into the office. It was Ramirez! Like always, my mom must have called him the second she knew something was

16

wrong with me. No wonder he hadn't answered his phone.

"Who did this? *Who did this?!*" my mother yelled, brushing my hair and then hugging me. Her eyes were wet and bloodshot. I didn't want to see them. I pushed her away.

"Ma, I need to talk to Officer Ramirez now. It's important. Can you all leave us for a minute?"

Mr. Mitchell and Ms. Spencer stared at each other. My mom started shaking her head, the way she always does before she says no. I looked at Officer Ramirez. I needed him to listen to me.

"Please, Imelda. It will just be a minute," he said.

Mr. Mitchell almost looked hurt for a second, but he walked out of the office without a word. So did Ms. Spencer. Officer Ramirez closed the door behind them.

"What happened, Martin?"

I closed my eyes and took a deep breath. I was about to do something I never did before—talk to a cop. For a second I couldn't speak, like invisible hands were holding my mouth shut.

Snitch! I could hear a voice in my head insulting me. *Martin Luna's a snitch!*

That's one thing you don't do in the barrio, something I never did no matter how many times I got in trouble. But I kept thinking of Huero and what was about to happen in his name. I couldn't let it happen.

"I know who shot my brother," I said, careful to keep my friends' names hidden. "His name is Hector Maldenado, and he lives at 2187 Tanner Street. You need to throw his butt in jail before something really bad happens to him."

"Bad?" Ramirez said, studying my face. I knew he understood me. "How soon?"

"Like right now," I said, glancing up at the clock. "Get someone over there now, or it's gonna be too late."

"How do you know this?"

I shrugged my shoulder.

"Is Frankie Pacheco behind this?"

"I didn't say that." I knew I didn't have to. He was smart enough to figure that much out himself.

"Martin, if something happens to Hector, you and Frankie—"

"I didn't do nothin'!" I said before he could go any further. "And nothin's gonna happen if you leave right now. Go!"

My head felt like it was breaking apart. If you told me a month ago that I'd send out the police against my friends, I would have been all up in your face. Now look at me.

I just kept picturing Frankie and the boys rolling up on Hector only to have a dozen cop cars surround them. Either the cops would arrive early and catch Frankie with guns in his car, or they'd arrive too late and Hector would be shot.

Either way it played out, it was going to be bad. And I was at the center of it.

Martin Luna's a rat. That voice in my head wouldn't shut up.

Officer Ramirez bolted out of Ms. Spencer's office like someone whose house was burning down. Within seconds, Ms. Spencer, Mr. Mitchell, and my mother were back.

"What's happening, *mijo*? What did you tell him?" my mother asked, staring at me, her face pale like she was coming down with the flu or something. I felt sick too. Nauseous.

"Don't worry about it, Ma," I said, rubbing my forehead where Frankie clocked me. I could feel the lump there. And the blood in my hair. The pain.

My mother looked at my hands and

turned to Ms. Spencer. "Where's the doctor? How come you're all standing around? His head's bleeding!"

"The ambulance should be here any second, Ms. Luna." Ms. Spencer rubbed her own temples. She looked like she hadn't slept in days.

"Frankie did this to you, didn't he?" My mother gave me that look moms do when they think you're hiding something.

"It ain't like that, Ma," I said, my voice breaking. The less she knew, the better.

"The ambulance is out front," Ms. Bader called out.

"C'mon, *mijo*. Let's go. I'm going to ride with you."

I tried to stand up, but my balance was gone. The room spun like the inside of a washing machine. Even the fluorescent lights overhead became dim and hazy.

A paramedic got in my face and said something, but his words were slow and made no sense.

In the chair across the office, I noticed something strange.

A small boy, younger than any freshman. He was wearing a backwards Los

Angeles Angels baseball cap, and he was looking at me and smiling.

It was my little brother.

I'm so sorry for all this, Huero, I tried to say, but my words came out all mumbled.

"What did he just say?" the medic asked.

Tears filled my eyes. They burned as they snaked down my swollen face. I tried to reach out to Huero. To touch him again. But my arms were suddenly like dead weights and the world was fading around me.

I blinked and he was gone.

Then blackness . . .

I don't know how long I was out, but when I woke up, I was in a hospital bed wearing a papery gown. I felt naked and cold in that thing, but what woke me up even faster was the person at the foot of my bed.

It was Officer Ramirez.

"What happened?" I asked, sitting upright. I noticed my mother's jacket draped across a chair at the foot of the bed. My clothes were there too.

"You're in the hospital, Martin. Whoever hit you gave you a concussion.

You got a few stitches too, but you're all right. The doctors wanted to observe you for a while before they send you home. Now that you're awake, they'll probably get you outta here soon. Your mother's been here all day. She just went down to get a cup of coffee."

"But what happened with Hector? Did you get there on time?"

"Nothing happened, Martin," he said, crossing his arms on his chest. "We had people on Tanner Street, and I even had someone check out Frankie Pacheco's house . . . just in case," he said, eyeing me. I didn't blink. "He was working on his car when we found him. He kept at it all day."

My heart was pounding so loud I thought he could have heard it if he listened. *Nothing happened.* That meant I stopped them. Frankie changed his plans because of me. But what else did it mean? Was Frankie just giving up? And what about Hector? Was he in jail already? The questions flooded my head faster than I could speak.

"Listen, Martin. I want to applaud you for contacting me. Every day bad things happen in the city that could be prevented if someone were brave enough to take a stand. People complain all the time, but few are willing to step up and do something about it."

I ignored him. I wanted answers, not a pep talk.

"What about Hector? You got him, right?"

"Now listen, Martin," he said. I could tell by the way his voice hung in the air that he was going to say something I didn't want to hear. "We don't have any real proof that Hector did anything. He has no record, and he seems to spend his time with his family. Are you positive he shot Huero?"

I blinked. I couldn't believe my ears. Not again. Not another day with Huero's killer walking free.

"I know for a fact he did it," I blurted out.

"What proof do you have?"

I could feel my temper building. The truth was I hadn't seen anything that day except a white car with tinted windows. The only reason I knew Hector was involved was because Chago and Frankie told me. I knew they wouldn't lie, not about this, but I couldn't say that without bringing them into it. That would just make things worse.

"I just know he did it," I said.

"Well unless you can prove it, or you can get someone who knows to talk to us, we can't do anything except investigate. We can't just go arresting people on rumors, Martin."

His words were a slap in my face. After months of waiting, I couldn't listen to more excuses. For a second, I saw red. Blood red.

"*You see!* This is why people don't come to you. 'Cause when they do, no one believes them and nothin' gets done. I don't know why I even bothered with you. You're no different than the rest of them."

"C'mon, Martin. No one wants to solve your brother's murder more than me—"

"*I* do!" I screamed. "You think I took this beating for nothin'? It coulda all been different, *Officer*," I said, twisting the word into an insult. "If I'da known this is how it would end up, I wouldn'ta said nothin' to you." It was like a dam burst in my head, and my anger was just spilling out. I kept thinking about Huero. I saw him in my mind lying on the ground again, his life pouring through my fingers and dripping onto the

24

concrete like red rain.

"You know *we* got ways of handing this without the police," I added, unable to stop myself. I knew my words sounded like a threat, but I didn't care.

"Now be careful, Martin. You did the right thing today. You had enough guts and sense to try to solve this the right way. Now stick with it. I don't want to find you on the street in a pool of blood, and I don't want you to waste your life in jail. You're a good kid, and your mom would do anything for you. You've got more going for you than a lotta kids out there. Stay at Bluford. Get your education, and do something with yourself. You hear me?" He put his hand on my shoulder like we were friends or something.

"Yeah, I hear you," I mumbled, shrugging off his hand. Who was he to tell me what I should be doing when he let a killer go free? "I hear you sayin' you're not gonna do nothin' about what happened to Huero."

He looked like I had just slapped him in the face. Part of me wanted to hit him too.

"Look, there's no point talking to you right now," Officer Ramirez said, taking a deep breath and turning away from me. "I'm going to keep my eyes and ears open, and we'll be watching Hector. We're not giving up on Huero."

"Whatever," I hissed, cursing under my breath. It was like old times, when anger was the only thing I felt.

"And listen, Martin," he added as he reached the doorway. "No matter what you do, stay away from Frankie. He looked like he expected us to be watching him today. He might even think you were the reason we were interested in him. I'm saying this to warn you. Stay away from him, and if he starts bothering you in any way, call me. You got it?"

"Yeah, I'll call you," I said, knowing I would never do it, not after this.

He sighed and walked out. I grabbed my clothes and changed out of the hospital gown. Not only was my little brother's killer still out there. Now Frankie, the guy who used to be like a big brother, might be coming after me. And the only person in his way was Officer Ramirez.

Please! He was useless. A bull's-eye painted on my chest would protect me better than him.

"*Mijo!* Thank God you're awake. You've been asleep for hours," my mother said, rushing in from the hallway to give me a hug. "Did you see Nelson?"

"Yeah. He just left," I said.

"I'm so proud of you for talking to him. He's been so good to us. I hope you thanked him for what he did."

Thanked him? *For what?* I wanted to say. Getting Frankie after me and letting Huero's killer go free? I didn't feel like fighting with her in the middle of the hospital. My head still hurt, and I was tired.

"Whatever, Ma," I said.

She sighed and put her hands on my face, forcing me to look at her.

"You scared me," she said. "If Nelson wasn't with us this morning, I would have lost it. He told me you did a brave thing and that I should be proud of you. Now I don't know what happened, and since you won't talk to me about it, I'm just going to say this once. I don't want you hanging out with any of your old friends. They're no good, Martin. I don't want you going back there anymore, not unless you're with me."

"*What?*" I yelled, feeling my old temper coming back. "That ain't right. What are you punishing me for?"

"I'm not punishing you, Martin. I'm

protecting you. I lost one son, and I'm not gonna lose another one. End of story."

"You don't know what you're talking about. Neither does Ramirez," I yelled. My world was crashing down, and everyone I knew was trying to make it worse.

"You can yell all you want, but you're not going to see them anymore," she said.

"Yeah, we'll see about that," I mumbled just loud enough for her to hear.

She glared at me, and I just looked away. I knew she was serious, but so was I. Huero was buried in our old neighborhood, and if I wanted to visit him, there was no way I was going to ask for permission. Not from her or anyone.

I was glad when the doctor came in and cut off our conversation. He checked my head and shined a light in my eyes.

"I'm gonna send you home tonight," he said. "But for the next two weeks, be gentle with your head. That means no gym class, no sports, and *please*, no fighting. Another shot to the head could cause permanent brain damage."

He spoke as if I had a choice about where Frankie hit me. My mother sighed at his last words, but I ignored her.

"Whatever you say, Doc," I replied.

It was getting dark when we finally left the hospital. My mother and I didn't speak to each other at all on the bus ride back. What was I going to say? All I wanted to do was yell.

When we stepped off the bus, I walked ahead of her to our apartment. As I neared our front step, I spotted something dark covering our doorknob, something that made my stomach drop and my heart race.

My black bandana.

I grabbed it before my mom noticed it. But I knew who had put it there. The same person who knocked it off my head earlier that day. The same one who wanted me to know I was in trouble.

Frankie.

Chapter 3

That night I didn't sleep.

I kept listening to the creaks and groans of our apartment, wondering if someone was watching us.

It's funny how many sounds the night makes, especially when you're nervous. At one point, I swear I heard someone walking in our kitchen. I even grabbed Huero's old baseball bat in case I needed to hit something.

Just some pipes in the wall making noise. I checked all the closets and then glanced out our living room window to make sure Frankie's LeMans wasn't out there. Nothing.

Somewhere far away, sirens screamed, and a memory of Huero's ambulance ride to the hospital flashed in my mind. My mother and I followed in a neighbor's car, and we could see paramedics pumping Huero's chest through the small ambulance window. My mother screamed like she was being tortured. It was a real-life nightmare, worse than anything I ever dreamed. I shook off the memory, closed our blinds, and headed back to my room.

In the hallway, my mother had set up a tiny table beneath an old picture of Huero. Two red church candles were burning under the photo. I could see my brother's face dimly in the dark. It was like he was watching me.

"I miss you, little brother," I whispered to his picture.

The last time I whispered to Huero was on a night last spring. He had a bad dream, and he came into my room and woke me up.

"Martin, I'm scared," he said, his eyes half closed.

"Don't worry," I said to him. "Ain't nothin' in a dream that can hurt you." He yawned and rubbed his eyes. It was as dark and quiet a night as it ever got in our neighborhood.

He fell asleep next to me, and I was awake the whole night because he snored loudly and kicked me a few times. I was annoyed with him then, but now I'd do anything to have that time back. You're gonna have a moment like that too, a time when you wish for things to be back the way they used to be, even if they weren't perfect.

In the flickering candlelight, shadows crept up and down the hallway like ghosts. I remembered the boy I saw in the office at Bluford just before I passed out.

Was it Huero?

It might have just been the hit to my head. Maybe I was losing it.

Or maybe he was still with me somehow. Watching over me the way I was supposed to watch over him.

I'm so sorry I didn't protect you, little brother.

At 7:00 my alarm blasted me awake like it did every other morning. Only this time, I felt like kicking it. I must have slept an hour or two at most. The last place I wanted to go was Bluford High School.

Homework? I couldn't remember what my last assignment was even though it was just a day ago. When you're trying to survive, schoolwork is the first thing you drop. Teachers never seem to understand this.

On my way to school, I passed the parking lot where Frankie split my head open. Seeing it gave me the chills. And I got that gnawing feeling too, the one that tells you something bad is about to happen.

I looked around just to make sure Frankie wasn't following me. I kept picturing him standing at my front door, my bandana in his hand. The same hand that held a gun to my face. He wasn't anywhere in sight. Not yet.

At Bluford, I climbed the steps and noticed a few students looking at me funny. One kid was staring right at the stitches along my hairline.

"You got a problem, homes?" I said. The kid shook his head and walked away. "Yeah, that's what I thought."

Inside it got worse. It seemed everyone was secretly eyeing me as I walked down the hallway.

"Yo, that's the dude who got kicked out of his old school for selling drugs," someone whispered.

"Don't mess with him. He might be packin'," someone else mumbled.

Listening to them, you'd think I was one of the terrorists the FBI was always hunting. Rumors in school are like that, spreading like a fire no matter how false they are.

At my locker, I spotted someone familiar coming down the hallway toward me. Vicky. What was I going to do about her? With Hector and Frankie on the street, there was only one answer, and I hated it.

Vicky and me met my first day at Bluford. I noticed her the second I stepped into Mr. Mitchell's English class. He was in the middle of telling kids not to be late when I walked in with my attitude. My timing was so perfect that a few kids busted out laughing, and I played along. Vicky smiled, and when I saw her I almost forgot how angry I was that my mom had dragged me across the city to Bluford.

"Excuse me, sir, you have a guest," Steve Morris said, pointing me out to the teacher so he could get a laugh from his friends. I knew right then I didn't like him.

For a second, everyone stared at me like I was from another planet, like they never saw a kid from the barrio before. At Zamora High, almost everyone was brown like me. Bluford was the opposite, more black kids than anything else, although there were some Latinos, Asians, and a few white kids mixed in. If you ask me, Vicky's the finest Latina in the school.

I ended up sitting behind her and found myself daydreaming about her soft brown skin and the way her black hair spiraled down her back. Even her laugh sounded pretty. Like music, if you can believe that. My boys would never stop teasing me if I told them this.

"What's up with you, homes? You gettin' soft now that you're sweatin' that Bluford girl," Chago would say. It was true. Dude shouldn't talk, though. When his first girlfriend broke up with him, he got drunk and cried. I never told Frankie because he would have made a big joke out of it. He was cruel like that.

Mr. Mitchell put me and Vicky in a group to go over a homework assignment. We had to write an essay about heroes. Both of us ended up writing about someone in our family. Vicky wrote about her grandmother who died, and I wrote about Huero. I gotta admit it was the first time schoolwork ever helped me meet a girl. But it's true. When we read each other's papers, something clicked.

That Saturday, we spent the whole afternoon together. We walked in the park and grabbed some pizza. It was like one of those corny TV shows. But it was nice. For once, I wasn't the troublemaker who kept getting in fights, the son who almost hit his mom, or the thug about to throw his life away. Instead, I was Martin Luna, the person Vicky liked.

I had such a good time I felt guilty, like I was lying about who I really was. I even tried to tell her about it. It was the first time I was so honest with a girl.

"Vicky, you and me, we're different from each other," I had said, looking for the right words. "Really different."

"*So?*" she said. "What's that mean?"

"It just seems like you shouldn't be here with me," I told her. My face burned when I spoke. If she knew me and my homeboys were planning to shoot someone, she'd never even look at me. I hated being so dishonest, but how could I tell her the truth?

She touched my hand then, just for a half a second. My heart skipped.

"Martin, when I first saw you I was like, 'Oh no, who is this boy, acting so hard?' But when you wrote about your brother, you seemed so sad. That's when I decided I wanted to talk to you."

For an instant, I thought she was feeling sorry for me, and I nearly walked away just like that. I don't want any girl's pity. I ain't no one's charity case. But she stopped me.

"It's not like that," she said, pushing her hair behind her ear so she could focus on me. She rested her hand on her neck for a second. I couldn't take my eyes off her. "It's like you're more real than the guys around here."

I couldn't tell what was real anymore, but I knew I wanted her to always feel that way about me. And in a way, I understood what she was saying. Compared to other girls I knew, she was more real too. Deeper.

But who was I kidding? After what happened with Frankie, everything was different. We had to end things.

I took a deep breath as Vicky approached my locker. For the first time since we met, I didn't want to see her. Don't get me wrong. It's not that I don't like her. It's the opposite. I like her too much to let her get tangled in my mess.

"Martin!" she said, stopping just

37

behind me. "Are you okay? I can't believe you're back in school." I watched as she struggled not to stare at the stitches on my forehead. "I was so worried about you."

Her words burned my insides, like she was poking deep into my chest with a hot iron. Looking at her dark hair, her soft skin, and her concerned eyes, I knew I had to get her as far from me as possible.

Don't think I'm crazy. It's what I learned from Huero's death. If I'd kept him away from me and Frankie, he wouldn't have been on the street when the bullets were flying. It's a mistake I won't make again. The bandana on my door told me everything I needed to know. The only way to keep Vicky safe was to keep her away from me.

"I'm fine, Vicky. Just a little bump on my head. No big thing." I shifted my books and tried to hide what I was thinking. She stared at me oddly, her eyes intense and focused like twin spotlights on my face. I wished I could hide myself from her gaze, but there was nowhere to go.

"You scared me yesterday. All I could think about last night was your face and that cut on your head." She shook as if the image in her mind hurt her some-how.

"C'mon, Vicky. You know I'm hard-headed. It takes more than a little cut to keep me down." One of my books slipped out of my hand and slammed down to the locker floor with a loud crash.

Vicky jumped at the sound and took a deep breath. Overhead the first bell rang, and people in the hallway started rushing off. We had two minutes to get to class. Two minutes for me to force myself to act this way.

"What happened yesterday? You have to tell me."

"Just an argument that got a little out of hand. We're cool now, though," I said, picking up the textbook and trying to act calm. "It ain't nothin' to worry about."

She stepped back and cocked her head like I just insulted her. I pretended to organize some things in my locker.

"What's wrong with you, Martin?"

"*What?*"

"You're acting different."

"I'm sorry, Vick, but it's been a crazy time for me. There's just a lot of things I need to sort out right now."

"You wanna talk to me about it?"

I looked at her, and for a second I didn't know what to say. Of course, I wanted to talk to her. I wanted to listen to her, and part of me wanted to kiss her right there in the hallway.

But the best thing I could do was to get her to walk away from me, and the only way to do that was to make her want to leave. Asking her wouldn't work. She was too stubborn for that. I learned that when Steve Morris and his football player friends jumped me on the street.

"Just leave, Vicky," I told her when he and his boys climbed out of his car. "Go!" I yelled. But she didn't budge until my crew showed up and she knew I was safe.

It was all too close. She coulda been punched or stabbed or worse, and it would have been my fault. I couldn't live with myself if that happened. If it meant I had to lose her to protect her, so be it.

"We gotta get to class," I said, acting like she meant nothing to me.

Her jaw dropped.

"I don't understand. What happened to you? Did that bump on the head make you forget Saturday, you know, the day we spent together in the park?"

40

"I remember everything, Vicky. What do you want me to say?" I asked bitterly. "It's not like it was *that* special. It was just a walk, that's all," I lied. The truth was that it was the best day I had since Huero died.

Vicky shook her head at me.

I'm so sorry, girl, I wanted to say. *But it's for your own good. Frankie's coming. You gotta stay away from me.*

The second bell rang loudly. We had a minute to get to class. Vicky was never late before, but I could tell she would be today. It was all my fault, but what could I do?

"You're being such a jerk right now. What's your problem?"

I got more problems than you know, I wanted to say, but I bit my tongue.

"The only problem I have right now is you, Vicky," I said and turned away, hating myself.

I left her standing in the hallway alone.

Chapter 4

"It's about time, Vicky. I told you he's no good. I don't know what you saw in him in the first place," said Teresa, Vicky's closest friend. I could hear them talking in the hallway as we made our way to English class. Several hours had passed since I told Vicky off. They couldn't see me in the crowd behind them.

"You don't even know him—"

"I know he's nothing but a wannabe gangbanger, and that's all I need to know," Teresa said, cutting Vicky off.

Since we met, Teresa did nothing but give me dirty looks. I usually gave them right back 'cause I have no time for snobs.

"That's why he got beat up, 'cause he's a jerk and no one likes him," Teresa scoffed. "I guess he's not so tough if he got beat up that bad. You're better off without him."

I bit my tongue and kept my mouth shut, but it wasn't easy. If Teresa wasn't trying to cheer up Vicky, I would have told her off right there in front of everyone.

"Whatcha talkin' 'bout, Teresa?" cut in Roylin Bailey, a boy who sat in the back row near me in class. "I heard Martin clocked your boy Steve in Mr. Dooling's class. I'da paid cash money to see that," he added.

"Boy, you should save yo' money so you can buy some sense," said Tarah Carson, this heavy girl who knew everyone at Bluford. "Besides, it ain't none of your business, so just stay out of it."

"Can you *all* just drop it?" Vicky snapped as the group reached our classroom. I felt bad she had all this attention, but there was no way I could stand up for her. It would only make things worse.

"Drop what, Vicky?" asked Steve Morris. He came from the other side of the hallway and surprised her.

"Just forget it," she replied, rolling her eyes and darting into class. I was seconds behind them walking into the classroom.

43

Teresa was the first person to spot me entering. Her face twisted when our eyes met, like she just looked at a pile of garbage.

"Aw, c'mon, Vicky. Why you gotta be that way?" Steve said as I made my way to my seat. He glanced at me as I sat down, his eyes narrow and angry.

My problems with Steve started in gym class. I watched him slam into this short kid Eric who was playing him strong on the basketball court. Afterward, Steve boasted like he'd beaten Lebron James one-on-one. The rest of the class laughed along even though Eric was hurt. Just like at Zamora, it was the cowards who laughed loudest.

"It don't take much skill to hit someone half your size," I said, sick of listening to Steve show off. People in the locker room looked shocked, like I was supposed to be scared just because he's Bluford's star running back. Forget that!

The next day, Steve and his boys sucker punched me. I didn't even see them until I was on my back staring up at Steve's smirk. I couldn't let it end like that, so I followed him into the locker room and clocked him. That's when I got busted for fighting.

At first, no one told Ms. Spencer I hadn't thrown the first punch. But then Eric and Vicky came forward and told her the truth. Ms. Spencer kicked Steve and four other guys out of this week's football game. If you ask me, that ain't even punishment. Who cares about missing a stupid game?

But football's a big deal at Bluford, and Steve cared. The next day, he came at me again. Me and Vicky were walking down the street when this car whipped around. Next thing I knew, Steve and the four other guys surrounded us. It was five to one, and I was getting nervous, when Frankie and our crew pulled up in his LeMans.

"Hey, homes," Frankie barked as he got out of his car. "You ain't havin' a party without us, are ya?" He then spit a nasty white glob on the ground at Steve's feet.

Steve and his friends looked like they were about to wet their pants. It would have been funny, except Frankie had that sick smile on his face, the one that told me it was about to get ugly. He was going to put someone in the hospital—or a body bag. That's when I jumped in.

"He ain't worth it," I said, holding

Frankie back just long enough for Steve and his crew to get away. I knew things between me and Frankie would go downhill after that, but I just couldn't watch him ruin another kid, not in my name. Not after everything with Huero.

Steve wasn't about to thank me for saving his butt, though. I could see that in his eyes as I sat in Mr. Mitchell's class. Even though he was talking to Vicky, he was looking at me like he was planning something.

"Like I said, Steve, just drop it," Vicky replied. She started to look back toward me but then stopped herself.

Steve's jaw tightened up. His leg was twitching like he was ready to pounce. Up until I came along, he and Vicky were friends. They even went out for a few months last year. She told me it was no big deal, though Steve's eyes always said it was.

"Oh, so now you're not talking to me?" he asked, glaring at Vicky and then at me. "Don't tell me you're still into Sanchez. He's just gonna drag you down, girl. Like my grandfather used to say, if you lie with dogs, you're gonna end up with fleas."

"Awww *snap!*" Roylin shouted. "That's

cold, yo. He said Martin's got fleas!"

My blood started boiling. I was trying to hold on, to let it end this way so Vicky would move on. But I was having trouble. My fingers were purple from squeezing my desk.

"Don't do this, Steve," Vicky said.

"Do what? Tell the truth about your new boyfriend?"

"He's *not* her boyfriend," Teresa said. "She hasn't seen anyone since you two broke up."

"I don't need you to speak for me!" Vicky snapped, flashing an angry glare at Teresa.

"What's the matter, Vicky. You and Sanchez get in a fight?" Steve asked, a smirk on his face. "That must be where he got all them nasty bruises on his face. Or maybe those are flea bites."

I couldn't sit there anymore.

"You got somethin' you wanna say to me?" I asked, jumping out of my desk. My chair fell backward with a loud crash, but I didn't care. Teresa's jaw dropped like she'd witnessed a crime.

"You better be careful, *homes*," Steve replied, a smug grin on his face. "No one's gonna protect you in here. Not like last time."

Anger raced through my veins like fire. The truth was *I* protected *him* from Frankie. He knew it, but he was putting up a front, saving his reputation. I shoved a desk aside and moved toward him, my fists clenched, my pulse pounding like a drum in my forehead.

"Martin, don't!" Vicky yelled.

I ignored her. In my head, I could see myself smashing the smile off his mouth, breaking his nose. For a second, it was like the whole world had tilted, driving me toward him. Like he was the reason my life had fallen apart. Like hurting him would make it all better.

"*Martin!*" A deeper voice shouted, snapping me from my thoughts. It was Mr. Mitchell. He'd come into the classroom without us noticing. "Get back to your seat. *Now!*"

Dozens of eyes focused on us. Some people, like Vicky, were concerned. But most seemed hungry to watch a fight. You know how school is.

Steve stared at me with a cold, hate-filled smile.

"Whatever," I said. I walked back to my desk, grabbed my chair, and sat down. My ears were ringing and my hands shook with anger, but I held it in. Barely.

"I will see you after class, Martin," Mr. Mitchell said and then quietly began taking attendance. The class sighed, and people slowly turned to face the front of the room.

I took a deep breath, grabbed my notebook, and tried to swallow down the rage that still smoldered in my chest.

"Revenge is sweet," Mr. Mitchell said then, pausing so his words hung in the air. "Is this a true statement? Is revenge a good thing?" he asked, eyeing Steve, me, and the rest of the class. It was one of his trick questions. Everyone looked around for a second to see who was brave enough to answer. I didn't move.

"Definitely," Steve spoke up. That grin was on his face again. He even looked over at me. "If someone wrongs me, I'm gonna do what I gotta do to teach him a lesson."

"Okay," Mr. Mitchell replied. "I think a lot of people would agree with you, Steve, although Vicky doesn't appear to be one of them," he said turning to her. Her hand was raised, and she looked annoyed.

"But when does it end?" Vicky cut in. "I mean if someone does something to you, and you do something back. Then the person just wants to get back at you, and it goes on forever. How does that solve anything?"

Steve was silent for a second. "Hey, I'm just bein' real. That's just the way it is. If people can't handle it, they shoulda never started trouble to begin with," he said.

"But what if someone gets in your face when *you're* doing something wrong? Are you going to get revenge then when it was *your* mistake that started everything?" Vicky cut back, her words sharp as blades. Though she said no names, I knew she was talking about how I called Steve out for hitting Eric. "Oh, I forgot, *you* don't make mistakes."

Some students laughed. Even Steve smiled with a look that said Vicky proved her point. I loved seeing her in action. Her almond eyes were so intense you could almost feel heat from her stare.

"Easy, Vicky," Mr. Mitchell said. "What Vicky is showing us is that revenge can be messy. Very messy. What we are about to read in this class is a messy revenge story. One which involves lies, betrayal, violence, even murder—"

"Sounds like a day in the 'hood,"

Roylin said, and a few students laughed.

"Nope, it's *Hamlet*, a 400-year-old play that is as rough as anything we've seen in the movies or read in this class."

A few kids rolled their eyes as Mr. Mitchell started passing out books to each of us. *The Tragedy of Hamlet, Prince of Denmark* by William Shakespeare. I flipped through my copy. It was filled with old-fashioned words like in my mother's Bible. *Thou* and *thine*. Who can read that stuff?

The word *Hamlet* seemed stupid to me too. Like the name of a sandwich or something. But the way Mr. Mitchell described it made it seem interesting. A revenge story involving a murder. It sounded too familiar.

The next thing I knew, Mitchell had the class reading a scene out loud. There was this ghost of someone who had been killed. He was begging for his son Hamlet to catch his murderer.

"*Avenge me*," he said over and over again. Even though it was 400 years old, I knew the meaning of the words. I lived them every day when I thought about Huero and the coward who shot him.

At the end of class, I was reading ahead, slowly connecting the strange words like pieces in a large puzzle.

"Martin, what happened today?" Mr. Mitchell asked as soon as the class emptied. He closed the door so no one could hear us. His voice was almost angry. I didn't want to hear a lecture, not after Steve started with me. That boy was asking for it.

"Huh?" I said, playing dumb.

"Don't give me 'huh,' Martin. I'm done playing with you. You are skating on thin ice in this school—"

"*So?* You think I'm just gonna sit there and let someone diss me? That ain't hap'nin'."

"Martin, listen to me for a second. I'm talking to you man-to-man now."

"Oh, so now we're gonna be friends? Wassup, homes! Go ahead, Mr. Mitchell. Let's be *for real*," I snapped, unable to stop the anger spilling from my lips. I know it wasn't his fault, but I just couldn't take it. My mom, Frankie, Vicky, Steve, and now him. It was just too much.

"Martin—"

"What do you want me to say? *Sorry, Mr. Mitchell,* I was wrong to stand up in class. Next time I promise to sit there like a punk and let him bust on me," I said, checking my anger before it went too far. "Look, Mr. Mitchell. I gotta go."

He did something that struck me then, something that hurt.

His eyes dropped, his shoulders slumped forward, and then he nodded.

"Go," he said quietly. "Get out of here."

That second, he looked defeated. It was like I had truly exhausted him. I knew I was pushing him away, but I guess I was testing him, hoping he wouldn't give up, trusting that someone still believed in me. Anyone.

You are talented and have potential, Martin, he had said the other day. I held those words like a lifeline when Frankie was hitting me. They led me back to Bluford, made me contact Officer Ramirez, gave me hope that there was more for me than streets where brothers die.

"Maybe you were wrong about me, you know, what you said the other day." I could feel my anger thawing for a second, sense the ocean of sadness beneath it.

"No, Martin, *you* are wrong about you," he said, rubbing his forehead. "Wrong to blame yourself for things that aren't your fault. Wrong to keep pushing people away, wrong to let stupid comments from Steve

53

jeopardize your career here at Bluford. Wrong to protect guys that aren't your friends."

I couldn't speak or move. My feet were nailed to the floor, and my mouth was glued shut. He was dropping truth on me like a rain of bombs.

"You're wrong about *me*, too," he added. "I'm not here to punish you or make your life difficult."

"I guess *you* got all the answers then," I replied, kicking my foot against my desk.

He took a deep breath. "No, I don't, Martin, but I know some of what you're going through. My nephew was killed by a stray bullet in a drive-by shooting nine years ago just a few blocks from this school. He was only six years old," he said resting his hand briefly on his chest like he was saying a prayer.

I couldn't believe what I was hearing.

"The police never found the person who did it, and to this day, I think it's because people are too scared to talk," he said.

I could feel him watching me. I kept my eyes focused on a crack in the tile floor. Anything to avoid his gaze.

"I'm sorry."

"I see too many kids taken down on these streets, Martin. Too many young people swallowed up by drugs, guns, and gangs. Kids who don't know better making bad choices that ruin their lives. I decided a long time ago to try to catch kids before they fall. It's one reason I became a teacher. I'm sayin' this so you know where I'm coming from in case you want to talk."

"You think I'm one of those fallen kids, don't you? That's why you're always in my face?"

"No, I think you've got a difficult choice to make. Right now, you're still standing. But if you get kicked out of this school, where will you be? Another fight and that's what will happen."

I glanced up at him. "School is the least of my problems."

He nodded. I could hear students lining up in the hall outside his door. His next class was about to start.

"Martin, we both know you know a lot more than you told the police the other day. As someone who has lost someone, I need to say this. For your brother's sake, you've got to tell the police what you know. I know it doesn't sound right, but if you keep one kid safe because you get a gun or a criminal off the street, it's worth it."

Mr. Mitchell had been making sense until he started asking me to snitch on my friends. Then I started feeling pressure in my head. Like my skull was crammed full of tangled knots. I needed to get away from him.

"Next period is about to start," I said, getting up from my chair and heading toward the door. "I gotta go."

He sighed and followed me to the doorway. "Remember what I said, Martin. You have a choice to make. My door's always open if you ever want to talk."

I nodded and rushed past him into the crowded hallway, never looking back.

The last class of the day was gym with Mr. Dooling. Thanks to my doctor's note, all I did was sit on the bleachers and watch everyone play basketball. Steve, Clarence, and the rest of their friends dominated the court, but they weren't pushing anyone around, not even Eric. He nodded to me from the other side of the gym.

It was the first time I'd seen Eric

since my fight in the locker room. I wanted to smack him for talking to Ms. Spencer. Yeah, it was brave, and it got me out of trouble, but so what? Where I come from, talking to the principal could get you beat up—or worse. I couldn't handle him getting hurt for me.

"Eric," I said, walking up to him after class. "We need to talk, bro." He smiled when he saw me, a look that reminded me of my little brother. For a split second, I almost forgot what I was going to say.

"Wassup, Martin. You all right?" he asked, glancing at the cut on my head. "Man, what happened to your face? It wasn't Steve, was it?"

"Don't worry about it," I snapped, angry that he was still looking out for me. "Look, Eric, I heard about what you said to Ms. Spencer. You need to stay out of my business, homes. You hear me?"

"What's your problem? I just told her the truth."

"I don't care what you told her. Just stay out of it. What you did was stupid." I felt guilty saying the words. It was like back in the day when I scolded Huero for following me and Frankie. But if I'd only been harder on him, maybe he'd still be here today. I wasn't making that mistake again.

"*Stupid*? I was sticking up for you. The only thing that would be stupid is if I let you get busted when you didn't do nothin'. If you think that's the kinda friend I am, you got me all wrong." His brow was creased and his eyes were focused. He meant what he said.

That's what scared me. I couldn't handle another person being in danger because of me. Another person I might not be able to protect. The next thing I knew, I heard myself blurting out words I never meant, words I shouldn't have said.

"Who you kiddin', Eric? We ain't friends. You can't even take care of yourself, so you got no business worryin' about me," I said, giving him a shove to make my point. "From now on, just stay away from me, and stay out of my business."

"What's your problem, Martin? What'd I do to you?" he said, not even trying to defend himself.

I wished he'd insulted me or called me a coward for being too scared to be his friend. But he didn't. Instead he just stood there, looking hurt and confused. I couldn't stand looking at him like that.

Without a word, I turned and stormed out of Bluford, glad to escape the place that felt more like my prison than my school. I'd only gone two blocks when I spotted something that made my heart drop to my feet.

It was Chago. He was watching me from across the street.

Chapter 5

"Yo, homes, wassup?" Chago said, lighting up a cigarette. His words seemed normal, but his face was pale and tense, like he was about to throw up.

I glanced up and down the block to see if he had come with Frankie, but there was no blue LeMans anywhere.

"Wassup, Chago," I said, eyeing him cautiously.

He took a long drag of the cigarette and blew a cloud of smoke into the air. I could smell the stink from across the street.

When we were kids, he and I used to hang out all the time. In junior high, we started messing around with cigarettes and beer like the older kids. I hated that stuff. The smell, the taste, the cost. But Chago was different. In eighth grade, he discovered weed, and for a while, that was all he wanted to do.

To pay for it, we stole things. A car stereo here, a bicycle there. No big deal, but it wasn't right. I remember how I had felt when Huero's bike got stolen, how I wanted to beat up the kid that did it. And then one day I became that kid. It's all ancient history now.

No matter what stupid things we did back in the day, me and Chago were always tight. He would always tell you what he was thinking straight up, and since he and I were cool, we never had any problems. Not like me and Frankie. You know all about that.

"Martin, we need to talk, homie." His voice sounded forced and unnatural, like someone had a knife stuck in his back.

"Tell me something I don't know," I replied, double-checking to make sure we were alone. "Where is he?" Chago knew exactly who I was talking about.

"He ain't here, Martin. Not yet," he said, crossing the street. "He doesn't know I'm talking to you, and to be honest, I can't believe I am either."

He tossed his cigarette butt onto the sidewalk, pulled out another one and fished around in his pocket for a lighter.

He smoked whenever he was nervous.

"Man, you keep smoking like that, and you're never gonna be an old man, Chago," I said. I knew how silly the words sounded, like the warnings you see on cigarette packs. When you're just trying to get through today, you don't even think about tomorrow. "Besides, you smell bad enough already without them nasty things."

He laughed, but there was nothing happy about the sound. Like the laugh you have at a funeral when you recall something funny about the person who passed away.

"Remember how we used to run up and down the street when we were kids? When playing was all we had to worry about?" Chago said, carefully putting the cigarette back into the box and kicking the curb with his shoe. I'd seem him do that a thousand times whenever he was thinking.

"Yeah, I remember. That was a long time ago."

"I wish we could go back there," he said.

"Me too, homes. I'd give anything just to go back to last summer."

Chago winced. I knew the words hurt

him. Of all my friends, he was the one who liked Huero most. He cried with me at the funeral, and he wanted revenge as much as I did.

"Frankie's pissed at you, homes," he said suddenly, changing the subject. "I ain't never seen him so mad."

I nodded. I expected as much. "I know. You think I'm stupid?"

"I don't know what to think about you anymore," Chago said with a sigh. "You used to be one of us, and now look at you. Frankie says you punked out and ratted on us to the cops, like you wanted us arrested or something. Ramirez been all over us for the past two days."

"Man, all of you been smokin' too much. You know I ain't like that. I never said Frankie or anyone's name to the cops. You believe me, right?"

Chago shrugged. I could see that Frankie had worked hard to turn him against me. "Then why did Ramirez stop by checking us out like we did something?" he asked.

"'Cause Frankie left his signature on my face. Ramirez ain't stupid. He knows somethin's up." Chago nodded. He knew I was telling the truth.

On the street, cars slowly passed by. One driver, an old white man, eyed us as he approached the corner where we were standing. He even locked his car doors as he waited for the light to turn, like we were carjackers or something. I almost said *Boo* just so he'd stop staring. Chago spat on the ground as the light changed and the car raced away.

"So that's it then? You just walkin' away from us and leavin' Hector on the street like nothing happened? What about Huero—"

"What *about* Huero, Chago? The bullet that killed him was meant for Frankie. If I had stayed away from him, Huero would be riding his bike right now, not lying in the ground," I said, forcing the tears back.

Chago wiped something from his eye. We were both quiet for several seconds.

"I understand you hurtin', bro. All of us are. That's why we gotta get revenge. C'mon, homes. Let's talk to Frankie. He'll probably be cool with you if you come around now. From what I hear, Hector's at his crib tonight. Tanner Street ain't that far away. Let's do this like we said back in the day," Chago urged. "Let's do it for Huero."

Chago's last words caught me like a nail catches your skin. He acted like killing was the best way to show respect for a kid who never hurt anyone, who smiled at strangers and felt sad whenever he saw a stray cat. That's not my brother's way. Huero wouldn't want me to shoot anyone. He wouldn't want me abandoning Mom and wasting my life in jail either. I figured this out one afternoon when I cut class to visit his grave. No matter what Chago, Frankie, or anyone said, I had to *live* for Huero—not kill for him.

"*I'm* takin' care of Hector myself, Chago. *My way*. I don't need you or Frankie's help to do it," I snapped. It was true, though I wasn't sure how.

"Homes, you ain't thinking straight. We been tight for years, so I'm gonna tell you straight up. If you walk away like this, you're gonna make Frankie an enemy, and you'll be alone against Hector," Chago said. "It's like a street fight. The dude in the middle gets hit from both sides. You can't survive that."

"Then I won't survive," I said. "We all gotta go sometime, Chago. At least I'll see Huero again."

Chago glanced at me and then

turned away. I'd seen him act this way before, when he disagreed with me but knew there was no changing my mind. Like when I stopped buying him weed 'cause I thought he smoked too much.

"Why don't you take off?" he said suddenly. There was something desperate in his voice. "You know, run away or join the army or something. Just until Frankie cools down. Those recruiter dudes are all over the place these days."

I almost laughed in his face at how crazy his words sounded. You gotta admit, it's a messed-up world when going to war is safer than staying home.

"I'm serious, Martin. Go away for six months, a year," he added, almost like he was begging me. Chago had never given me advice before. Usually he was asking for it about girls, or work, or dealing with his mom. Frankie and I used to tease him about it. But things were different now.

"I can't leave, homes," I said. My mother and I had already moved across the city. And at 16, I wasn't joining no army. Besides, I couldn't leave my mother alone, not after what she'd been through.

Chago was about to try and argue

with me. I could see it in his face, but I cut him off.

"So is Frankie comin' for me, Chago? Is that why you came down here?" I asked.

Chago reached into his pocket and grabbed the cigarette he'd just put away. I knew the answer before he opened his mouth.

"You know Frankie. He don't take 'no' from anyone."

For several minutes, we stood on the corner and said nothing. Chago finished his cigarette, tossed the butt onto the sidewalk and looked back at Bluford.

"And what about you, Chago? Will you be with Frankie when he comes?"

Chago shook his head and cursed under his breath.

"It isn't supposed to be like this. We're brothers," he said finally, sadness in his voice. "C'mon, Martin. You were always the smart one. Can't you think of some way out of this? At least try makin' it right with Frankie. Try talkin' to him."

"Look at my face, Chago. This is what happened last time we talked. I got nothin' to say to him."

Chago sighed and played with his lighter, making the flame flare up and die back. I almost felt bad for him, the position he was in. But that's the way the world is, puttin' you in bad positions and forcing you to make a move. Like Mr. Mitchell said, you have to make a choice.

No one ever said choosing was easy.

"He got your mom's schedule from his sister, Martin. He knows she's working late this weekend. Saturday night. That's when he's coming, when you're alone," Chago said, his eyes like storm clouds. "You didn't hear this from me." He turned and started walking back across the street.

Watching him, I knew Chago was still my homie. He made a choice by risking his neck to warn me. It was more than many people would have done.

"Thanks for coming down here, Chago," I said as he left. His head was down, his eyes low. He didn't once turn back.

From now on, I was on my own. And Frankie was coming.

My head was spinning as I made my way home. Frankie was going to make a lesson of me. In a way, he had no choice. Everyone would think he was soft if he allowed me to stand up to him. People would start talking. His reputation would suffer, and then younger wanna-be's would push and test him to get respect. I'd seen it before. He had to prove to the rest of our crew that there was no questioning him.

But how far would he go? At the least, he'd give me a beating I wouldn't be able to walk away from after a day. Maybe worse. I remembered the doctor's words just before I was discharged from the hospital.

"Another shot to the head could cause brain damage."

I knew what another fight with Frankie would be. More shots to the head. Harder ones.

"I ain't never seen him so mad." Chago's words echoed in my head.

This time Frankie would be more brutal than ever. I kept picturing the way he kicked the kid at that party. The horrible wet crushing sound it made. Frankie would give me the same treatment. No, he'd give me worse.

By the time I made it home, fear was digging at me the way rats clawed through the walls of our old apartment. My mother was still at work, and it was dead quiet as I walked in and locked the door behind me. From the shadows at the end of the hall, Huero smiled at me from his picture.

"I might be seeing you again soon, little brother," I said crossing myself the way we do in church.

Getting beaten isn't what scared me most. I'd been through that enough times as a kid with my father. Once, when my mother was pregnant with Huero, my dad got drunk and started swinging. She fell trying to get away from him, and I jumped in between them.

"Stop it, Papa! You're hurting her," I screamed.

He hit me so hard my teeth pierced my lip like glass ripping through an old trash bag. I was on the floor in a puddle of blood when he left in a storm of English and Spanish curses. That was one of the last times I saw him. Eight years ago, and I still have a scar on the inside of my lip from the stitches, his only lasting gift to me.

At the time, my mom called me her hero, saying I protected her and my brother. But she never understood that it was *fear* that pushed me, not bravery.

Fear that if I didn't act, I'd lose them. Fear that I'd fail to keep my mom and brother safe.

Huero's death made those fears real, turned them into wounds that hurt worse than any bruises Frankie could give and scared me more than any threats.

Pacing in my apartment, I felt these fears again, driving me like hunger. If Frankie was coming for me, if he was going to bring everything he had against me, I wouldn't survive. But there was something I needed to settle first. A problem that would make my life a complete failure if I didn't solve it. One that would turn me into a restless ghost if I died before I could finish it.

I looked at Huero's picture and knew where I had to go. It was not about Frankie or Chago or Bluford. It was about Huero and the person who shot him.

Time was ticking. Frankie was coming. Ramirez had done nothing. I needed to move while I still could. I needed to find justice for my lost brother.

The next thing I knew, my feet were taking me away from our apartment to the bus stop on our corner. Without a word, I boarded the bus to Tanner Street.

To Hector Maldenado's house.

Chapter 6

It was about 4:30, and the October sun was still high overhead when I stepped off the crowded bus onto Tanner Street.

I'd been to the neighborhood a few times before. Huero had one of his little league games with the Police Athletic League in a park just off Tanner Street last year. Ramirez was an assistant coach with the team. That's how he and my mother met. Huero played center field.

Frankie and I had also been through the area in his car a few months ago when we were looking for Huero's killer. Frankie said he had a girlfriend that used to live not too far from the park. I remember the conversation because it was funny.

"This girl was so fine, homes. But she was bad news too. She used to hide knives in her hair just in case," he'd said.

I laughed because Frankie had no room to say anyone was trouble. He was the one with the gun hidden under his seat.

"She had to be trouble to put up with you," I said at the time.

"It's true. If I had a daughter, I'd never let her near me," he said. "You neither, homes. You're a mess," he joked, gunning the LeMans back home.

Tanner Street was a lot like my old neighborhood. Just a 15-minute bus ride from Frankie's house, about 40 minutes from Bluford High, the area was all Chicano.

Small one-story stucco houses faced each other on both sides of the street, some with little gardens, a few with statues of *La Virgen*, the Virgin Mary. Many houses had iron bars on the windows too, just like our old place.

Leaving the bus stop, I spotted a mural on the side of a nearby garage.

Increase da Peace, it read in faded silver and black letters the size of a person's chest. Beneath the words, the artist added an image of a maroon lowrider cruising in the sun, chrome wheels sparkling like diamonds. Between the words and the car, two giant brown hands were painted as if they were coming together in a handshake. If you didn't know better, you'd think the neighborhood was safe, that peace was on the march.

But more recent than the mural were the gang tags painted on the walls of nearby buildings. One even covered a corner of the mural, an insult to the art and its message. I didn't recognize the name, but I knew it was a sign of who was in charge. Hector's house was up the street. My fingertips started tingling, and my palms got sweaty as I moved closer.

If my mother knew where I was, she'd never let me out of the house again. And if she had any clue what I was doing, the tears would be flowing down her face in full force.

"If anything happens to you, it will kill me, *mijo*," she'd wail.

Truth is, I didn't know what I was doing as I walked up the block. Dogs in houses on both sides of the street started barking at me. Brown kids with faces like mine stopped playing to look at me as I passed by. On a nearby porch, I saw an elderly couple watching me. They were all people who knew not to trust strangers walking in their neighborhood, but there I was.

Chago's words were ringing in my ear.

"The dude in the middle gets hit from both sides. You can't survive that."

But I couldn't stop myself. It was like I was possessed as I marched up the block and spotted the homies outside 2187 Tanner Street, Hector Maldenado's house.

There were four guys standing next to a blue Ford pickup parked on the street. Another dude was behind the wheel, and other people were in front of the truck, though I couldn't tell how many because the hood was up.

"Homes, you ain't never gonna get that thing to start," said one guy without a shirt. He had a beer in his hand and a tattoo of a spider's web on his right shoulder. I could see it from halfway down the block. He was my height but bigger and more muscular.

"Man, give César a chance. He fixed it last time."

"Yeah, but that was before . . . you know."

"Yo, why don't you shut up about that, man? Show some respect."

"Relax, homes. I'm just bein' real, that's all."

"No, you're bein' real stupid."

I was close now. Maybe about ten yards away. If they weren't all looking at the truck, they would have noticed me walking right up the sidewalk. I still don't know what I was thinking or planning to do. Just looking for answers. For proof. A reason.

Maybe I was looking for something else too. An ending. I don't know.

"Try it now," a voice yelled from the front of the truck.

The dude behind the wheel turned the key, and the old Ford came to life in a cloud of blue smoke that I could have hidden in if I were smarter or saner.

"I told you'd César would get it working. Your brother's still got his skills, Hector."

"That's 'cause I'm the one who taught him," came the response.

My heart was racing as I stepped closer. I needed to see their faces if it was the last thing I ever did. I was just

ten feet away when I first heard footsteps behind me.

"Yo, homie, whatcha looking for? I
hope it's a bus stop 'cause this ain't your
'hood."

The whole crew surrounding the
truck suddenly turned to face me.

"You know him, Hector?" the dude
behind me asked.

Two guys came around from the
front of the truck then. One of them, a
stranger to me, was standing, wiping
grease off his hands with a rag. The
other appeared a second later in a
wheelchair. I knew his face.

In my head, I was at that party again.
I was watching Frankie lean over a guy
who was on the ground, hearing the
thud of his boot as it slammed into the
poor dude's stomach, dodging the foamy
vomit as it poured onto the floor at our
feet. The guy had looked up at me a second before the impact. Burned his face
forever into my mind. I'd seen it many
times in nightmares since the fight, but
it was never in a wheelchair. Never with
legs so thin and weak.

"No, I don't know him," said Hector, the
guy holding the rag. He stepped toward
me. "You looking for trouble, homes?"

My eyes were still locked to that wheelchair. I nearly went down right there in the street.

Please tell me it's not true, I told myself. But in my heart I knew it was. No one could have walked away from what Frankie did that night. Me, Chago, and the rest of the crew knew it, but we never said anything. Instead, we pushed it back. Buried it.

But some things can't be buried.

For a second, I was frozen. Paralyzed. The answers I searched for since Huero's death came crashing through my skull like a gunshot. It started with César and Frankie talking trash at the party. Then Frankie took it too far. He crippled César with that kick. Hector wanted revenge. He came after Frankie and found him on my block.

But Hector's aim was off.

And bullets don't have names. They cut down anyone. Everyone. Even eight-year-olds who are in the wrong place at the wrong time.

My legs suddenly felt weak. My stomach started churning. Before me were Huero's killer and Frankie's victim. One boy dead. Another in a wheelchair. And for what? I wanted to scream.

For what?!

Respect? Revenge? *That ain't nothin'!* Neither could fix César's legs, bring Huero back, or empty the graves of all the fallen kids lying in them now.

The world was spinning, and I felt like it was about to fling me off like a piece of garbage. Another life lost in the barrio, just like my brother. Another world crumbled into dust.

"Are you high, homes? You musta got some bad weed or somethin'," the big guy said with a laugh.

"I don't like the looks of him. Is he packin'?"

In an instant, hands were all over me, searching for a weapon I didn't have, one I knew I couldn't use even if I held it in my hands.

"He don't even have any money. You know he's gotta be usin'," someone said.

I got shoved to the ground and landed on my backside in front of a group of guys who were my enemies but didn't know it. They were no different than my old crew, and one of them had suffered too, would suffer for the rest of his life from the looks of things.

It was all too much. I felt like a blister about to pop. I had to get away, or I was gonna lose it. But if I told them the truth about who I was, it would be the end of me.

"I'm lost," I said to them. It was all I could say.

"You damn right, you're lost. You're in the woods now, homes."

"Man, I told you he's high. *Vato loco.* Stay away from whatever he's smokin'!"

"Five-O," someone yelled then, and the crew backed away as a black and white police car pulled up next to us.

"Again? That's the second one today," someone else added. I knew the reason. It was because of what I told Ramirez. I was sure of it.

"Is there some kinda problem here?" I heard a different voice say, though from the ground I couldn't see much. Then a car door opened.

"No problems, Officer," the big dude said. "Hey, why don't you pick up our trash for us. This boy's as high as a kite."

I looked up to see a white police officer, maybe in his early 30s, sizing me up like I was a crime scene.

"You okay, son?" he said slowly like I couldn't understand him. "I see your eyes are red. Have you been smoking something I should know about?"

It was the same old deal with the cops in the barrio. Here they were in front of a killer and didn't know it. And here I was with my eyes red from tears, and I'm accused of using drugs. I've said it before, I'll say it again. The world is messed up.

"I just need to get home," I said.

"Let's take you to the station first," he said, helping me into the back of the police car. Funny how my first time in a cop car was the one time I hadn't done anything wrong.

The crew watched as the cop pushed me into the backseat. César had wheeled around close and studied me, his stare cutting me deeper than any blades.

Tears rolled down my face as the car started moving. The questions that had haunted me for months suddenly had painful answers.

"You sure you're okay, kid?" the officer asked, eyeing me in the rearview mirror.

I shrugged and stared out the window. There was no way I could tell him what was going on inside me, the sudden twisting I felt deep in my bones. Like

I was an old rag and someone was wringing me out, wrenching me from the inside.

"I don't know what you're hiding, but you're one lucky kid," the officer said. "We just increased patrols on this block this week. If you'da been here before today, no one would have found you."

"Yeah, I'm *real* lucky," I said wiping my eyes. I knew my talk with Ramirez was the reason the patrols were added, but I didn't say anything. The officer had probably saved me, but I didn't care. Sitting in the caged backseat of the police car, I didn't feel lucky or saved. I felt cursed.

Hours passed before my mother finally arrived at the station. By then, she was so upset that she could barely look at me.

"I don't know what to do with you anymore, *mijo*. My manager at work is upset with me because I keep leaving work early. And if I miss another day, we're gonna have trouble paying the bills. I keep praying, but I can't seem to get any answers," she said sadly as we walked into the apartment close to 10:00 p.m.

Just seeing her made me ache

inside, but I didn't have any words that would make her feel better. I didn't have any for myself.

She wiped her eyes and shook her head. I was standing in front of my bedroom door. I hadn't told her or anyone what I saw. How could I explain that I felt like a bomb had blown out all that remained of me after Huero's death?

My mom started praying then, turning to the candles and the picture of Huero.

I closed my bedroom door, shut out the lights, and felt hot tears crawl down my face in the thick darkness.

Chapter 7

Suddenly I was on my hands and knees.

Struggling. Unable to move. Something tight was looped around my neck.

I look down and see black cords stuck through my arms and legs. Holding them like chains. I look up and see a giant web. Like the one in the tattoo on Hector's friend.

I was caught in it.

Nearby are two bodies I recognize. Huero and César. But further out there are more. Countless others I don't know. An endless sea of bodies, gray and still in the dark. Their eyes are closed. But mine are wide open. We're stuck in the web together.

I try to free myself, but I can't move. There's no sky and no ground. Just *blackness swallowing us like the ocean.*

I scream but no sound comes from my mouth . . .

"Wake up, *mijo*. You're dreaming." Mom's words startled me out of my sleep.

I sat up and threw the blanket off my arms as if it was the web that held me. My T-shirt was soaked with sweat. My heart was pounding.

"What is it, *mijo*?" my mom asked, turning on the light next to my bed. "Are you okay?"

"I'm fine, Ma," I said, wiping my face and taking a deep breath. "Just a crazy dream."

She sat at the foot of my bed. Her tired, bloodshot eyes looked like two cracked windows. Since Huero died, she seemed ten years older. And my troubles only made her age faster.

Watching her, I wished I could stop the suffering I caused, go back and redo that night at the party, or change that afternoon last July when Huero died. Mr. Mitchell was right to talk about choices, but all the ones I made were wrong.

I'm so sorry I put you through all this, Ma. I wanted to say, but the words didn't come. Instead, I just looked at the clock to avoid her eyes. It was 3:33 a.m.

"You never smile anymore, *mijo*," she said then. "I hardly remember what your smile looks like."

"You neither, Ma."

She nodded and wiped her eyes.

"You're right," she said, putting her hand on my arm. "When you and Huero were babies, I swore I was going to give you both a better life than the one I had. Nothing was more important. Now . . . " she paused, tears slipping down her face. "I just think I failed you. Failed my two babies."

I couldn't stand to hear her blame herself for my mistakes.

"It's not your fault, Ma," I said, forcing myself to look into her weary eyes. "You weren't on the street with Huero that day," I said, feeling the sorrow in my chest. The guilt. "He was with *me*."

"No. Don't do that, *mijo*. I see you walking around with the weight of the world on your shoulders, blaming yourself. You're not a parent. It's not your job to keep your kids safe. That's a mother's job," she said.

I don't care what she said. I knew more than she did about what really happened to Huero, how I could have

87

prevented everything.

I hugged her then because I didn't know what else to do. She held me and cried, each tear burning my insides hotter than any fire.

"I'm sorry I snapped at you last night, *mijo*," she said finally. "I know you are missing Huero too. It's just that I get so worried."

"It's okay, Ma," I said. I felt so bad for her. She had no idea about Frankie's visit or the trouble that was brewing. And I didn't have the heart to tell her.

"Martin, listen to me. I know I yell at you a lot, but there's a reason for it. It's because I love you. No matter what you think you did or what you blame yourself for, know that I love you. There is nothing more important in this world to me than you."

I felt the tears in my own eyes then. Tears of sorrow and guilt. Tears of fear and worry.

"I love you too, Ma," I said. "No matter what happens."

She hugged me again, though I could see the concern on her face. Something about my words unsettled her. It almost felt like a goodbye.

Maybe it was.

Three hours later, I was walking to Bluford. I hadn't slept after the talk with my mother, and I couldn't stand laying in my bed and staring at the ceiling, my mind racing with images I wished I'd never seen.

César crumpled on the ground.

Huero bleeding in my arms.

Frankie's smirk.

I was so out of it when my alarm went off that I left home without a shower, without looking at the clothes I wore, without even grabbing my books. I just had to get out.

On the street, I followed a group of kids making their way to school. I could hear them talking about their classes, worrying about their grades, their homework assignments.

I know it ain't right, but I felt like slapping them because they were happy. Because they didn't look in the mirror each morning and hate what they saw. Because they could sleep at night knowing they hadn't destroyed their family. If I was Frankie, I would have done it.

At my locker, I was surprised to see Teresa standing there waiting for me. Her lips were tight, and she looked like she was being forced to do something she hated.

"Aren't you at the wrong locker?" I said to her.

Teresa sucked her teeth and rolled her eyes. "I don't know what Vicky sees in you. But I'm here 'cause she's my girl," Teresa said. "She's done nothin' but stick up for you since you got here, and you went and hurt her yesterday. That ain't right."

I cringed inside at her words. I knew I deserved the mean look she gave me, and I respected her for having the guts to stand up for her friend. She was right. Vicky did deserve better. That's why I pushed her away.

"I told her what she needed to hear," I said.

"No, you didn't. You were a coward who didn't even tell her anything. You need to step up and end it with her, so she stops worrying that there's something wrong with you. Just tell her it's over and show her what a jerk you are so she can move on."

I hated Teresa's voice, her attitude. The look in her eyes that told me she thought I was beneath her. But there was truth in her words that stung me.

Coward. Maybe I was afraid of being honest with Vicky. Afraid of what she'd really think if she knew what I was about. But even if it was true, it was none of Teresa's business.

"Girl, get outta my face. You don't know nothin' about me," I said reaching into my locker and grabbing my copy of *Hamlet.*

"I know you're the worst thing that happened to her. That's all I need to know," Teresa cut back.

I slammed my locker shut and headed down the hallway. I was supposed to go to biology, but I couldn't stand the idea of sitting in the class and talking about plant cells. What's the point of that?

Instead, I snuck into a far corner of the library behind the magazine racks and the computer tables. Another student bundled in a thick black jacket was asleep at a work table. I ignored him, grabbed a chair, and cut my next three classes.

During the time I cut biology, homeroom, and U.S. history, I read *Hamlet* and learned how he goes nuts planning revenge on his dad's killer, and then starts talking to himself and snapping at everyone around him. He even chases away the sad girl that likes him. I swear, it was like the play was talking about me.

I read so much, I decided to go to English class. As soon as Mr. Mitchell walked in, he announced a pop quiz.

"I hope everyone read the first act of *Hamlet* for homework," he said as he passed the quizzes out.

"Come on, Mr. Mitchell," Roylin complained. "Why you always gotsta do this to us?"

"If you know he always does it, it shouldn't be a surprise to you," Steve said. "Even Martin can figure that one out."

"Enough," Mr. Mitchell said. "No more talking until the quizzes are done."

Vicky turned and handed the quiz back to me. Our eyes met for a second. I wanted to talk to her, to explain, but I couldn't say anything. Not with Mr. Mitchell watching us.

The *Hamlet* quiz was easy. For the first time I could remember, I had no problem identifying who everyone was and what happened in the first act. In fact, I was the second person to finish the quiz.

"You okay, Martin?" Mr. Mitchell asked when I handed my paper in. "You sure you don't want to look over it again?"

A few kids snickered, like they couldn't believe someone like me could get the right answers. I looked back to see who was laughing, but no one met my gaze.

During the rest of class, I stared at the back of Vicky's head and tried to listen to Mr. Mitchell's talk about how guilt destroys Hamlet. But all I kept thinking about what was coming, what I still had to face.

Before class ended, I scribbled a note just in case.

Dear Vicky,

> *You're right to be angry at me. Right to think I'm a jerk.*
>
> *I'm dealing with a lot right now, and I'm not sure how it's all going to turn out.*
>
> *I didn't want to drag you into all my problems, so I thought the best thing I could do was push you away. I never meant to hurt you. Our walk in the park was the best day I had since I came here. Your smile kept me going.*

Martin

P.S.—Teresa may be a jerk, but she's got your back. If you see Eric, tell him I'm sorry.

I folded the note, and dropped it on Vicky's desk without a word. It was the last thing I wrote in Mr. Mitchell's class.

Just a few hours later, my time at Bluford ended.

Chapter 8

"Get off!"

I could barely make out the words over the noise of showers spraying and locker doors slamming. It was the end of gym class, and I was emptying out my locker when the voice spoke out from the back of the room.

"Let go of me!"

This time I knew who it was. Eric. Then I heard people laughing and a low thud.

I rushed out into the aisle that divided the locker room. Our gym teacher, Mr. Dooling, was on the far end talking to a couple of football players. I could tell they were trying to distract him.

The air was a soupy mixture of steam, sweat, and deodorant. It was the last class on Friday. Most students were rushing to get changed and go home, but a few stood nearby looking toward the back of the locker room. No one moved closer, though.

Cowards. I cursed under my breath.

I knew whose lockers were there. It was where I'd fought Steve after his boys jumped me. I dropped my gym clothes and headed straight back. I could hear voices growing louder as I got closer.

"I told you to keep your mouth shut, Eric. Next time you want to be a hero and step up for your boy Martin, you better think twice. 'Cause if you ever rat us out to Ms. Spencer again, it'll be the last thing you do. You hear me?" I recognized the voice. It was Steve's friend Clarence, a linebacker on Bluford's football team, whose neck was as thick as a tire.

I stepped into the corridor and found Eric doubled over. Two guys had his arms hooked behind his back, the same two guys who had grabbed me from behind last week. Clarence was in front of them, and I watched his big dumb fist fly into Eric's stomach. Steve was on the other side of them, looking down on Eric, who coughed and slumped to his knees. I could see tears in his eyes as he looked around desperately for help.

"I got kicked out of this week's game because of what you said to Ms. Spencer. You better hope this doesn't affect my scholarship chances, or you won't walk again," Steve hissed, spitting on the ground.

That's when I snapped.

Steve's threat and the sight of Eric slumped over sent me flying out of control like a train off its track. I slammed my fist like a hammer into Clarence's chin. Steve gaped in surprise when I turned and jabbed his nose, knocking him backward into the wall of lockers. The two punks holding Eric let go and stepped back, eying me like I was a dog ready to tear into them.

"*Fight!*" someone screamed.

Clarence came at me then, and I started swinging, cursing, kicking. Everything seemed to go by in slow motion, but I kept thrashing even after the teachers arrived.

I couldn't explain why I swung at every arm that tried to pull me away. Why I was unable to calm down as they yanked me out of the locker room. Why I shoved poor Mr. Dooling against a wall when he tried to break my grip of Clarence's neck, or why I fought the three security guards who raced into the locker room and wrestled me to the ground.

Everyone—teachers, students, guards, even the janitors—stared at me like I was a monster with horns growing out of my head.

"Psycho," Clarence said, rubbing his jaw as I left the locker room.

"You're *done*, Sanchez," Steve yelled with a cold smile on his face. "Outta here. Have fun in juvee."

"He's lost it. That boy is nuts," one guard mumbled as they dragged me down the hallway like I was some kind of criminal.

"Maybe he's strung out on something," another guard said.

I know it must have looked that way. I was trembling and shaking. My jaw locked shut, my pulse pounding, sweat dripping off my face.

There was no way I could tell them that seeing Eric on the ground reminded me of my brother. No way I could describe the white-hot rage that boiled in my chest at them. There were no excuses for what I did. But in that moment, there was no way to hold it back.

Almost 30 minutes later, I was in Ms. Spencer's office, my head down on the same desk I sat in during my first suspension. My heart was still pounding, but the red haze in the air was disappearing like morning fog.

My eyes were wet and puffy. I must have been crying, and my hands were marked and swollen with cuts from the punches I'd thrown. My T-shirt was torn too.

Ms. Spencer came carrying a thick folder with my name on it. She sat down on the opposite side of the table from me. The lines in her forehead seemed even deeper than usual.

"I'm sorry I lost it, Ms. Spencer," I spoke up first. What else could I say to her? It was the truth.

She opened the folder, leafed through some sheets and then looked at me. It seemed like a long time before she said anything. "I'm sorry too, Martin," she replied.

Outside I could hear one of the secretaries talking to someone.

"A troublemaker like that doesn't belong in this school. I wouldn't want my child in class with a boy who behaves like that. Someone could have really gotten hurt today."

"I knew he was trouble the second he walked into this school. He was nothing but attitude from day one," another woman replied.

I wanted to jump up and tell them off. What did they know about me? Nothing. Sure, it was wrong to lose it in school. But what about ganging up on another kid when no one is looking? Which was worse?

If you ask me, it seems most people don't know what really goes on in school. And if they did, a lot more of the kids would be in trouble. Popular kids, not just the ones everyone thinks are troublemakers.

"Martin," Ms. Spencer said, her voice heavy and slow. "You are in serious trouble for what happened today."

I nodded. At least she was being straight up with me. "I didn't mean to push Mr. Dooling, Ms. Spencer," I admitted right away. "I'm sorry I did that. It should have never gone that far."

"Well, it's good to hear you say that. And I'll be sure to mention it to Mr. Dooling, Martin. But what happened today is . . . there just isn't much I can do for you. My hands are tied."

"What do you mean?"

She took her glasses off and stared at me. "Martin, you've been in this school for only two weeks. In that time, you've been suspended. You've cut class several times. You've been involved in multiple fights, and today, you struck a teacher. It took three guards to bring you here. I can't have that behavior in my school. Parents, teachers, and my staff will not stand for it, and neither can I."

"I said I'm sorry. Look, I was standing up for Eric. They were hitting him. What was I supposed to do? Leave him by himself to get beat up? I couldn't do that, Ms. Spencer."

She wrote some notes on a pink piece of paper. "This isn't the street, Martin. It's a school, and it has rules which you broke. I warned you last time about controlling yourself, and today you were worse than ever. I'll look into what happened, but that does not change what you did today or what I must do now." Ms. Spencer dropped her pen, put the pink sheet into my folder and closed it quickly.

"What do you mean? What's gonna happen?"

She took a deep breath and studied my face for several long seconds. It was like she was looking for something to make what she had to say easier. "I hate to have to do this, Martin. To you and your mother," she began.

"What about my mother? What is it?"

"I'm afraid you are being expelled."

"*Expelled*? You mean you're kicking me out?" I asked, surprised at how much her words hurt.

She nodded heavily. "I'm very sorry, Martin."

I slumped back in my seat. The office was quiet for several seconds.

"Martin—"

"No, forget it, Ms. Spencer. It's all good," I said, trying to pretend I didn't care, but my voice was cracking. "I never belonged here anyway. Besides, I'm sick of you all gettin' on my case all the time. At least now I won't have to hear Steve anymore neither."

"Martin, listen to me," Ms. Spencer urged, leaning forward toward me. Every student who is expelled is given a ʼaring in front of Mr. Gates, the super- ʼndent. Yours will be next week. Go to ʼearing, and explain your side of the Maybe you can convince him to allow you to remain at Bluford. But for now, I have to follow school policy. There's nothing more I can do."

If I got the news a month ago, I would have been happy. I never wanted to come to Bluford in the first place. But deep inside I could see it gave me a chance I didn't have anywhere else. And then there was Mr. Mitchell and those words.

Potential. Talent. Promising future.

Getting expelled was like saying there was no hope for me. That my place was on the corner with the other guys who were being gunned down and who were doing the shooting. Even though it wasn't cool to say it, I started wanting more than that.

Too bad, Martin Luna. Now you're going back where you belong, Ms. Spencer seemed to say.

She's right, homes. Stop pretending you're somebody else. School's not your world. You belong with your family, Chago would say. But I'd burned that bridge, too. My world was collapsing. The end was coming.

"Yeah, I'll talk to him, Ms. Spencer. I'm sure he's gonna listen to what I have to say. Just like everyone else around

103

here," I said.

"Good luck, Martin," Ms. Spencer said with a weak smile. She wiped her eyes quickly and stood up.

I rushed out the front doors of Bluford High School for the last time, trying my best to hide the burning in my eyes. The angry tears that dripped down my face because another door had just slammed in my face.

It felt like a kind of death sentence.

Chapter 9

"*Expelled!*" my mother cried when she got home from work that night. I didn't even try to defend myself 'cause I knew there was no point. She wasn't going to listen to anything I had to say.

"I'm sorry, Ma."

"*Sorry?*" she yelled, her voice rising even higher, piercing my skull. "Is that all you have to say? That's not good enough. Sorry doesn't fix anything!"

"What do you want from me? I told you—"

"*What do I want?*" she repeated, cutting me off and moving right into my face. "What I want is for you to stop throwing your life away. Your principal told me you pushed a teacher. I couldn't believe my ears. 'Not my son,' I started to tell her, but she said at least ten people watched you do it. *Pushed a teacher!* Even at Zamora you never did nothin' like this!"

"Ma, I was standing up for my friend," I tried to explain. I needed her to understand that I wanted to do the right thing. That I didn't mean for this to happen. That no matter what happened, I wasn't a bad person. "I just lost it when—"

"Yeah, you lost it all right. You threw away everything. *Everything!*"

"Ma, you don't understand—"

"No, *you* don't understand. You're killing me! I can't take it no more. Everyday I go to work, I'm scared of what you're doing. Whenever the phone rings, I'm afraid to pick it up. One day you're in the hospital. The next you're in a police station. Then I get a call from your principal saying you got expelled. What are you trying to do to me?" she demanded, her words hitting me harder than any punches, breaking me up inside.

"But Ma, I told you it was an accident. I didn't mean to hit him. These dudes were hurting this kid and—"

"I don't want to hear it! I'm tired of you making everything so difficult all the time. And I'm tired of your excuses. No matter what happened, you could've handled it differently. Told a teacher. Talked to the principal. You had a choice. But what did you do? You went and started hitting."

I knew part of what she said was right, but she didn't understand what seeing Eric did to me. How it scraped open the wound of Huero's death. I was drenched in gasoline, and it was the match that set me on fire.

"I can't keep doing this, *mijo*. I'm getting too old," she said, heading down the hallway to her bedroom. Her voice became weaker somehow, like something deep inside her had broken. Had finally started to give up. "I moved us here to get you out of the barrio, to get you a decent education, and to give you a chance your brother will never have. If all you're gonna do is throw it away, shame on you," she said, taking a deep breath and wiping her eyes. "I need to go to bed. It's been a long day."

She walked past me into her bedroom and closed the door, leaving me standing at the edge of the dark hallway alone.

The candles beneath Huero's picture

cast the only light in the hall. I looked at his portrait and fought back the tears.

"I'm sorry," I whispered. To my mother. To Huero. To everyone I'd wronged.

But my mom's words echoed in my head, slicing me like switchblades inside, cutting me to the bone.

You're killing me . . .

Shame on you.

The words hurt so much I almost didn't care that Frankie was closing in like a pit bull ready to bite my throat.

Mijo,

> *I'm working late tonight for inventory. There are leftovers in the fridge. Nelson will bring me home. Call me if you need anything.*

I reread the short note my mother stuck on our refrigerator. Her words were cold and distant. I crumpled the paper and tossed it in the trashcan when I heard a knock at the door.

For a second, I imagined Frankie had come already. But when I looked through the tiny peephole, I saw Vicky staring back at me. She looked nervous. Suddenly I was too.

I thought about not answering the door. It was almost noon, and I hadn't even showered. I knew I looked bad, but I couldn't just leave her standing there. And part of me was grateful to see her.

"Wassup, Vicky," I said, opening the door. She was wearing a snug pink T-shirt and jeans, and she looked better than ever. Seeing her, I didn't know what to say. My tongue was all in knots. All I could do was be honest. "It's good to see you, girl. I can't believe you came here, though."

"You think you're going to keep me away with a note like this?" she replied with a smile. She was holding the note I wrote her in class yesterday. "When I read it, I was like 'Why hasn't he just been honest with me?'"

She was staring at me, her eyes friendly and sincere. In her gaze, I felt exposed somehow. It was like she could see right into me. Like she was looking at the guilt in my heart, the stupid mistakes I made, the trouble hanging over me like a curse.

"Look, I'm sorry, Vicky. I've just had a rough time lately. A lot of stuff has been going on, and I didn't handle it well," I admitted. I needed her to understand I never meant to hurt her. "I shouldn't have treated you that way."

"You're right, and if you do it again, you'll be sorry," she teased.

"I *am* sorry, Vicky. Seriously," I said.

"I know you are, Martin. That's why I'm here," she replied. "You think I'd come over here if I thought you were a jerk?"

"Girl, you're crazy. Just because I'm sorry doesn't mean what I said to you isn't true. You should stay as far away from me as possible." I meant the words, forced them out even though they hurt to say.

"Oh my God, I am *sooo* sick of hearing that. Look at me, Martin. I'm standing here because I like you. If you honestly don't want me around, just tell me, and I'll leave. But if I hear another person—especially you—tell me I'm doing the wrong thing, I'm gonna freak."

"How can you be so sure about me, Vicky?" I said, unable to hide the sadness bubbling inside me. I stepped away from the door so I could hide my eyes, but she followed me.

"'Cause if you were really a jerk, you wouldn't try so hard to protect me, Martin," she said, putting her hand on my shoulder. "If you were really a jerk, you wouldn't have stood up for Eric in the locker room. And if you were really a jerk, you wouldn't apologize to me neither. Believe me, I know what I see in you, and I'm sure I'm right."

I felt like someone who had been lost in the desert. Her words were like water. I wanted to drink them in, to believe them, but I knew better.

"But there's so much you don't know, Vicky." I was staring at the floor, shaking my head. Snapshots of all the things I'd screwed up flashed through my head. Huero lying on the ground. Frankie kicking César. Me hiding the truth from everyone.

"So tell me! That's what friends do, right?"

We were standing in my living room. The sun was shining outside, and there before me was this beautiful dark-haired girl who challenged me like no one else. I looked at her and just shook my head. I felt like I was standing on the edge of a cliff, and she was asking me to climb down to the bottom with her. My heart was racing. "I don't even know how, Vicky."

She glanced over my shoulder to the hallway. I knew she could see the candles and Huero's picture in the distance.

"Is that your little brother?" she asked, slowly stepping past me toward the hall.

"Yeah, that's Huero. The picture was taken about a year before . . . you know." I moved next to her, our shoulders touching.

"Oh my God, Martin. You two have the same eyes."

"You think so?"

"Definitely," she said, examining the picture. "He's cuter than you, though."

I almost smiled at her then. "He was the coolest kid, Vicky. You woulda loved him." It was the first time I'd ever really talked about Huero to someone that didn't know him.

"I believe it," Vicky said. "I feel like I know him a little bit through you, and I like him already." She smiled and placed her hand on my shoulder.

I felt like I was melting inside. Like my anger and sadness was a tight fist that she was gently opening.

"I miss him so much," I confessed.

She rubbed my back then, and I couldn't hold back. It was like cracks were opening inside me and pain was ready to pour out.

"Why couldn't I have protected him? Why did he have to die, Vicky?" My voice was shaking, breaking up, but the words kept coming. "Why wasn't it *me* that got shot?" I asked, trying to pull away from her. But she held me.

"I'm so sorry, Martin," she said, pressing herself into me. There were tears in her eyes.

"It should have been me," I said, my face burning with shame. I had never said the words, but they haunted me every day. Clouded everything I did since Huero died. Made me hate my own reflection and wish I'd never been born.

"No, Martin," she said, touching my face. "It shouldn't have happened to anyone. Not you. Not Huero. But you can't do that to yourself. You have to go on. That's all we can do."

"It *should* have been me," I repeated, tears rolling down my face, my chest beginning to heave. I didn't want to cry. I had fought it for so long, kept everything buried down deep. But Vicky's words, her touch, and her tears thawed me. "I wish it was me. . . ."

I wept then like a small child, felt the hurt like lead weights on my back begin to lighten slightly. Vicky hugged me the

113

whole time. I listened to her breathing and felt her heart beat against my chest. Twice she wiped her own eyes, the tears she shed for Huero. For me.

I don't know how long we stood there holding each other in front of Huero's picture. When we finally pulled away, my T-shirt was splotchy and wet from our crying. With anyone else, I would have been embarrassed, but not with her. We stared at each other for several long seconds without a word. Then she did something that surprised me.

She leaned forward and kissed me.

Her lips were soft and smooth. I closed my eyes and touched her soft face, ran a hand through the long spiral curls that stretched down her back, smelled the strawberry shampoo she had used to wash her hair.

We kissed just once, but we spent the rest of the day together. I didn't tell her about César or that Frankie was coming later that night. I was afraid she might do something crazy and get herself hurt for me. I couldn't risk that.

"You have to fight your expulsion, Martin. You have to go to that hearing and tell the superintendent everything," she said later that day when we were eating pizza at Niko's.

"There's no way he's gonna listen to me. Everyone who saw me thinks I'm a thug. I heard the secretaries talking about me in the office."

"Who cares what they think? They don't get it. You gotta make them understand and show them who you really are," she urged. There was this tiny crease in her forehead. I'd seen it in class whenever she said something she really believed in. Now it was there because she believed in me. I didn't agree with a word she said, but I wanted to kiss her again right there. She was as much a fighter as anyone I knew, and she was on my side.

"But it's not that simple, Vicky," I explained. She started shaking her head at me. I know she didn't understand what it was like to have everyone think you were a criminal, how you were guilty before you even opened your mouth. "Besides, I pushed Mr. Dooling."

"Well, if you don't fight this, shame on you 'cause I expected more from you," she said, putting her hands on her hips. I couldn't believe her words. The same ones my mother had said.

"Girl, this isn't even about you. Why

are you getting in the middle of it?"

"I am already in the middle of it. Steve's my ex-boyfriend, remember? And then there's you." She smiled, and for a half second she blushed. She knew what I was going to ask her next. I could see it on her face.

"And what am I?"

"That depends. What do you want to be?" she asked with a sly smile. My heart jumped. I grabbed her hand.

For the first time at Bluford, I had a true friend. And for the first time in my life, I had found a girl who moved my soul. It figures both came on the day I had to face Frankie. The day after I was kicked out of Bluford.

"I'll tell you later," I said, holding her hand, making a silent promise to answer the question if I ever got the chance to be with her again. If I survived my clash with Frankie.

She squeezed my hand back and smiled. She knew I wasn't telling her everything, but right then it didn't matter. I wished I could have bottled the moment. Saved it forever somehow. Because at that table in the back of Niko's, with Vicky's soft hand in mine, I felt something new. Something I'd lost months ago, maybe something I never really had.

I felt glad to be alive.

And yet, even then, I could feel Frankie coming to strip it all away. Snuff it out like a candle.

If there was going to be any hope for me in this world, I had to stop him.

Tonight.

Chapter 10

Alone in the apartment, I paced for several hours hoping what Chago said was wrong. That Frankie was not coming for me, and I wouldn't have to see him again.

At 10:00, after checking and re-checking each noise and every car on the street, I turned out all the lights. Maybe Frankie would leave if he thought no one was home. Or maybe the crew would convince him to grab some beers and chill somewhere.

But deep down, I knew I was kidding myself.

"*I ain't never seen him so angry.*" Chago's words echoed in my mind.

I had to face Frankie one last time. It was the only way I'd be able to look at myself in the mirror, silence the angry voices in my head, and honor my fallen brother.

By 11:30, the apartment was still quiet. I stretched out on my bed listening to the sound of each car engine outside.

Each siren racing off in the distance.

Each rustle of the restless mice in the walls.

Only the red numbers on my alarm clock and the flickering candles under Huero's picture kept the place from being as dark and quiet as a grave.

As my eyes grew heavier, I started thinking Chago had managed to talk some sense into Frankie. Told him to leave me alone, to let it all go. I was almost nodding off when I heard the step outside our apartment door creak strangely.

If it were my mother, I'd hear keys jingling, the locks opening with a solid click. Not this time.

First someone tried to open the front door of our apartment. Of course, I had locked it, but Frankie knew how to break a lock just as fast as he could break a nose. There was a heavy thud, then a pop followed by a quick metallic snap. A second later, I heard the familiar groan of the door opening.

My heart started pounding like a bass drum. My palms grew slick with sweat. I grabbed Huero's old bat and crept out of bed to the edge of the doorway, careful not to make a sound. The door was half open, so I hid myself behind it and peered through the tiny gap along the door frame.

I could hear footsteps getting closer. From the sounds, I guessed at least three people had entered the apartment. Maybe more.

My worst fears were coming true. Frankie had brought the crew with him. My boys from back in the day—Jesus, Junie, and Chago—were now my enemies, breaking into my house in the middle of the night like thieves. Allowing Frankie to push them too far.

They paused for a second in our living room and whispered. In the silence, I could make out Chago whispering.

"I don't like this. That's Huero's picture on the wall. This ain't right."

"You scared, homes?" Frankie challenged. I knew his voice anywhere. "You back out now, and the scariest thing you'll see is me."

"I don't think anyone's here, Frankie." I recognized that voice too. It was

Junie, a dude who usually spent Saturday nights smoking weed, not hunting friends.

"Check the bedrooms." Frankie ordered. He was always getting people to do his dirty work. A year ago, he would have sent me to check the rooms, and I would have listened. No more.

My hands were tingling. I needed to stop him somehow. Stop him before he stopped me. I prayed my plan would work.

Our apartment was small. Only about twelve feet separated the front door from my room, and I could hear someone coming forward.

I gripped the bat tight, feeling the sticky tape Huero had put on it last spring.

The floor outside my room groaned slightly as someone approached. Then I heard footsteps move into my mother's room. Through the tiny crack in the door, I could see the back of a figure standing in the hallway looking at Huero's picture.

I raised my bat. The person stood still for several seconds, took a deep breath, and pushed open my bedroom door.

It was Chago. In the candlelight, I could see his eyes glistening and wide open with fear. He was staring right at me like he'd seen a ghost. If it was anyone else, I would have swung the bat, but instead I raised my finger across my lips so he knew to keep his mouth shut.

"No one's in here," whispered Jesus from my mother's room.

"No one's in here either," answered Chago, looking right at me. I thought his whisper was too quick. Too forced. He turned and headed back to the living room, leaving the door slightly open.

I knew Frankie would break him if he found out about the lie. Chago knew it too. His forehead was covered in a thin layer of sweat that reflected dimly in the dark.

"You sure the place is empty?" Frankie asked, frustration in his voice. I couldn't see what he was doing, but I could picture him scowling at Jesus and Junie, making sure he could trust them.

"There ain't no one here. Let's get outta here before his mom comes back." Chago said. Someone struck a match then. Chago was smoking. I was sure of it.

"Why you in such a hurry, homes?" Frankie asked. I could hear the distrust in his voice. I knew what it meant.

The apartment got dead quiet. Frankie was whispering, but he kept his voice low this time. I couldn't understand a word he said.

"I told you he's not in there," Chago yelled suddenly from the living room. I bet he was trying to warn me.

Then I heard footsteps rushing down the hallway.

I knew I was in trouble. My arms were trembling with nervous energy. I said a silent prayer and peered through the crack in the door.

In the flickering candlelight, I could make out half of Huero's picture, but there was something unusual about it. A reflection of dim figures in the area under Huero's face.

The one in front was definitely Frankie. I could see his torso and head suspended in the air. As the reflections grew bigger, I saw something shimmer just for a second. Something metal.

It was like Huero was trying to protect me somehow.

I stepped back and raised the bat, knowing where I had to aim. Frankie's right arm. He was just outside my door. Only a few feet separated us.

All was quiet for a second. I crossed myself.

Then chaos.

The door smashed inward as Frankie kicked it with his steel-tipped boots, the same ones he used to cripple César.

I swung Huero's bat with all my might.

It sliced through the air with a deep, hungry *whoosh*, sailing toward Frankie's outstretched arm. I saw the pistol in his hand glimmer for a split second as the bat came crushing down.

Boom!

The air exploded with a blinding flash and the thunderous crack of a gunshot.

In the blast, quick as a lightning strike, I saw the bat crumple Frankie's right arm, bending his trigger finger backwards like a snapped pipe.

Then the room filled with the sour sulfur odor of gun smoke. My ears rang from the blast, but I still heard Frankie's screams, a sound that made the dark room seem like a torture chamber.

"My arm!" he hollered, rolling on the floor at my feet. "I can't move it."

I turned on the light, the bat still in my hand. Frankie's gun was on the ground next to him. I kicked it away as he struggled to get up. A hole in the floor next to my bed showed the harmless path the bullet took.

Chago, Junie, and Jesus were at the edge of the hallway. They looked stunned at the sight of Frankie holding his arm and me standing over him with a bat. Their world was suddenly turned upside down.

"You know what you gotta do," Frankie grunted at them, wincing at the pain. "Do it!" They looked at me and didn't budge. My ties with them were just as deep as his.

Deeper. We were all the same age, kids who grew up on the corner together. Frankie was the older one, a dude who used to push us around when we were little, someone who still pushed too much.

"Yo, homes, you need to get to the hospital," Junie said to Frankie. "Your arm is lookin' bad."

"C'mon, let's get out of here," Chago said, reaching a hand down to Frankie.

"No. He's not going anywhere," I said then. "You all can go, but me and Frankie got something to finish."

Frankie turned to me, hatred in his

125

eyes. I could see he was struggling with the pain. His arm was starting to turn blue.

"You feelin' brave with that bat in your hand, homes? Think you're gonna finish me off just like that?" he hissed, spitting at me. "I always thought you'd be the one to challenge me. But you're too soft. You don't have it in you."

Part of me wanted to finish it right there, the way it might happen on the street. A heavy swing of the bat, and I could end it all. His life. Mine.

Maybe you'd read it in the papers or hear it on the news. Another gang-related murder, the reporters would say, making me seem like a monster.

"Don't do this, Martin. C'mon, homes, just let him go," Chago said.

"Why, so he can come back and finish what he came here to do?" I said.

Chago shook his head. He didn't understand the lesson Huero's death, César's injury, and Mr. Mitchell's story taught me. That I had to break from the street before it broke me.

"Whatcha waitin' for, homes? I ain't got all day," Frankie challenged, his useless, broken arm swelling by the minute.

"The police," I said, hearing the first

siren in the distance. "I was going to call them, but in this neighborhood your gunshot took care of that for me."

Chago's eyes opened wide. Junie looked at me like I'd just spoken a strange language.

"I told you he ratted us out. He's a snitch. You're dead, Martin. *Dead!*" Frankie said, spit falling from his mouth.

"No, I'm more alive than you'll ever know," I yelled back at him, smashing the bat into the doorframe near his shoulder. The crew took a step back like I had a disease they could catch.

"I never ratted on any of you. Not after you crippled that kid at the party last year. Not after I found out that kid was Hector's brother and that's why he was shooting at us. Not after I figured out your stupid temper cost my brother his life and put another guy in a wheelchair. Not even after you put me in the hospital. No, Frankie, I never ratted you out. But I'm gonna do it now. You're going down, homes, and Hector's going with you. Huero's gonna have justice."

Something new flickered in Frankie's eyes then. It flashed for a second, and I'll never forget it. Fear. He glanced over at

Junie and Jesus, then at Chago. "C'mon, homes. Let's get outta here. I ain't waitin' here for no cops." He moved toward the hallway when I raised the bat again, blocking his path.

"You ain't goin' nowhere, Frankie," I warned. "This is it. You're stayin' here with me."

Chago backed away from him, looked at Huero's picture and then at me, and nodded. Jesus and Junie shook their heads and started walking away.

"You took it too far, Frankie. You always did," Chago said. "Later, Martin."

"Later, homes," I said as they walked out.

Frankie cursed, and in one swift motion tried to shove past me. But I jabbed the bat into his right arm, and he went down in agony.

"I told you this ain't done," Frankie hissed as he heard the sirens approaching. "It ain't never gonna be done between you and me. Remember that."

"No, it's done this time, Frankie," I said, looking at Huero's picture. "It's finally done."

For months, it had been a maze, but it all made sense now. I would tell Officer Ramirez what I saw at last summer's party. That would point the police to César and show them why Hector was shooting at us. They'd finally have the case they'd need to bust him. I'd make sure of it.

Huero's killer would be off the streets. And Frankie would pay, too, for crippling a kid and for coming after me with a gun. He might also have to answer to Hector's crew for what he did.

No matter what, my mother and I finally had answers. We'd finally have peace.

Frankie didn't say anything when the police arrived, but I showed them the gun and the bullet hole in my floor. Told them I used the bat in self-defense. I told them the truth.

My mother and Officer Ramirez rushed in as the police took Frankie away. For hours, I told them what happened, made sure Ramirez heard every detail. Watched him write it all down.

Maybe you'd have handled it differently, I don't know. But for me, there was no other way. If I didn't act, there'd probably be more dead kids right now. And I would have been one of them. I may still be one day. But not *this* day.

"Thank God I didn't lose you

tonight," my mother said over and over again after the police left.

"No, Ma. You didn't lose me," I said, feeling my eyes burn as the sun began to rise.

The wounds from Huero's death will never fully heal. The past will always haunt me. But there is a future too, a life I need to live—for Huero and for me. It's something I can't just toss away, not after all I've seen, felt, and lost.

"I'm still here," I said to her, feeling something new stir in my chest. A glimmer of hope.

"Thanks to Huero, I'm still here."

Mr. Gates grunts at the last words of my story, still hanging in the air like a prayer.

"Thanks to Huero, I'm still here."

He clears his throat. Overhead, the lights of the auditorium are beaming down. The room is crowded but suddenly very quiet. Even the rows of students, parents, and teachers are silent.

"Mr. Luna," Mr. Gates begins finally. "I want to thank you for having the courage to explain your situation to us tonight. I appreciate your honesty. This is a difficult decision. Does anyone have anything else to add on this matter?"

I hear people begin to mumble. Mr. Gates raises his eyebrows in surprise.

"Yes, sir. We do," says a familiar voice.

I turn back to see Mr. Mitchell. He's standing with Vicky, Eric, and a small group of other students. Some are wearing Bluford football jerseys, teammates of Steve's that I barely knew. I don't understand what's happening.

"Mr. Gates," Mr. Mitchell says. "I join a number of my students in support of Martin Luna. We know this incident was not provoked by Martin. While he may not have handled it well, we feel—"

"That won't be necessary, Mr. Mitchell, but I applaud you and your students for coming forward," Mr. Gates says, closing his folder.

I brace myself for the words that are about to crash down on me like boulders.

"In my time at this school, I have heard many stories from kids like yourself who are struggling in our school. It seems each year the obstacles our young people face get worse," he says, shaking his head.

"Now, Martin, I can see you are a sensitive and thoughtful young man.

And I am sorry for your loss and the troubles you've had to endure these months. However, I cannot tolerate the behavior you have shown since you've arrived at this school," he pauses.

The auditorium is silent for a second. I know his next words will knock me out of Bluford for good. I can barely breathe.

"*But*, given the details you've provided and what I've witnessed at this meeting tonight, I don't think expulsion is necessary at this point. You can remain here at Bluford High School, provided you meet weekly with the school psychologist, Dr. Boyd. However, if there is another incident this year, I will reverse my decision. Understand, Martin?" He's staring right at me, his blue eyes sharp and focused.

I feel dizzy. Is it true what he just said? Is he serious?

"Yes, sir," I blurt out. "Thank you, sir. Thank you."

The group behind me begins to clap, and I feel my mother embrace me, sobbing with joy. Over her shoulder, I see the people who came to the hearing and stood up for me. Snitches like Eric and Vicky, the bravest people I know.

"Thank you," I mouth the words to

them, to Mr. Mitchell, and then to the sky for Huero. I know he's up there somewhere watching, smiling down at me this very moment.

Mr. Mitchell was right when he said life is about making choices. I finally made mine.

I'm not perfect. I lose it sometimes, and I still have enemies at Bluford. But Huero gave me a second chance. For him, my mother, and me, I am going to take that chance and reach for the sky with it. That's my choice.

I tell Huero this as I look for him in the bright lights overhead.

"Oh my God, Martin. You did it," Vicky says as she runs over to me. I feel her hugging me as I squint up at the lights. "*You did it!*"

Tears start rolling down my face, and I let them fall away.

halfway there when the front door opened. It was Larry. He was carrying a Budweiser twelve-pack. I wanted to get up the steps before he came in, but I wasn't fast enough.

"*What are you doing here?!*"

Larry's voice boomed through the living room, and his face twisted in anger.

"I just wanted to get something to eat," I said, trying to calm him down. "I'm going back to my room right now." I moved toward the stairs, but Larry stepped in front of me, putting the twelve-pack down.

"When I want you upstairs, you *stay* upstairs!" he yelled.

"But I—"

Whap! Larry cuffed me hard in the jaw with the back of his hand, snapping my head back and splitting my lip. I could taste the blood in my mouth as I stumbled away from him, stunned.

Just get to the stairs, I told myself. I could hear him following me.

now, you're gonna wish you never met me."

He shoved me against the wall, and I scrambled away from him. Without a word, I raced up the stairs to my room and tried to lock my door to keep him out. But the old door barely fit in its frame, and I had to ram it shut. It seemed crazy to lock myself in the room, but what else could I do? I didn't want Larry anywhere near me.

About an hour later, I heard the front door slam. I looked out my window and saw Larry get in his old Dodge and drive off. It was past lunchtime, and I was hungry. I figured he'd gone back to work and would be out for hours, so I went downstairs to get something to eat.

Aunt Fay had bought us groceries to take with us when we moved, so the kitchen was already stocked with food. First I had a big bowl of corn flakes, and then I made a cheese sandwich. I was pouring myself a glass of orange juice when I heard a car door slam outside. I looked at the clock. It was way too early for Mom to get home.

My stomach sank.

I put my glass down on the counter and darted toward the stairs. I was wanna just hang out by ourselves. Maybe Donald and some of our friends will come over too, and we'll need space of our own. We're not gonna want a kid around." he paused to drink some beer. "Now you got a nice room upstairs where you can hang out, and I expect you to use it. You with me, *Benny*?"

Making me leave Aunt Fay and move into the beat-up house was bad, but now Larry was trying to boss me around too. I couldn't keep my mouth shut.

"My mom's paying half the rent here, so this is *my* place too," I blurted out. "And my name's *Ben*, not Benny," I added.

Larry snapped. He slammed down his beer and leaped out of his chair, grabbing me by the shirt. I'm five-eight and weigh 140, but Larry was at least six inches taller than me. His arms were solid like the black metal pipes in Aunt Fay's basement. He held my collar so tight, I almost couldn't breathe. For a second, I was helpless.

Get your hands off me! I wanted to say. But I couldn't speak.

"Don't you *ever* talk back to me, Bennyboy," he growled. "And if you don't get upstairs and outta my sight right the window. It made a clicking noise when I turned it on and worked only at slow speed.

I spent the rest of the day unpacking and trying to make the dreary room feel like home, but I kept hoping that Mom would change her mind and move back in with Aunt Fay.

It didn't happen.

The next day, I learned Larry's house rules.

It was mid-afternoon, and I was on the couch watching TV when I heard someone unlock the front door. Mom was working her usual shift at the day-care center and wouldn't be back for hours. I figured Larry, a plumber's assistant, had the same schedule. But when he came through the door, I realized I was wrong.

"How's it going?" I mumbled to him. It was our first time alone in the house.

"About time we had a chance to talk," he replied, shouldering past me to the kitchen. He came back a second later with a cold beer and grabbed the TV remote that I'd left on the couch.

"There are gonna be days when your mom and I get back from work and saying goodbye to Aunt Fay.

Mom and I followed behind them in Larry's car, and we drove to a rundown row house on Union Street, all the way on the other side of the city. On the way, she dropped another bomb on me.

"You're gonna have to switch to a new school, Ben. It's called Bluford High. Don't worry. Aunt Fay says it's a good school, and Larry says it's no big deal."

What does Larry know? I wanted to say, but I kept my mouth shut as he and Donald quickly unloaded our stuff. They barely talked except when Larry told him what to do or where to put things.

"You get the top floor," Larry grunted to me as I walked into the house for the first time.

He and Donald carried my mattress and old bureau up a narrow stairway that led to the third floor. I followed them, lugging up an old folding chair and a card table.

We entered a small room with a cracked window that faced out onto busy Union Street. The walls were a faded blue, streaked in some places with brown water stains from leaks in the ceiling. A larger back room was empty except for a rusty attic fan mounted in fights he'd gotten into at school.

"*I wouldn't be surprised if he did time somewhere, the things he and his friends used to do,*" Jackie admitted after seeing him pick up my mom one night. "*But that was fifteen long years ago, Fay. People change,*" she had said. Aunt Fay just grunted. They didn't know I was listening.

No matter what anyone said, Mom saw no problems with Larry. She ignored Aunt Fay's advice. Two weeks later, she made me dress up with a shirt and tie like we were going to church. Instead, we went down to the municipal building and got in a line with a bunch of other people. Then an old judge called us into a stuffy conference room, and my mom and Larry were married.

Just like that, I had a stepfather. He didn't look at me the whole time.

The day after the wedding, Mom and I packed our stuff into cardboard boxes and plastic trash bags. Larry came over around noon with a stocky, dark-eyed guy named Donald. Within minutes, they crammed all our things into the back of an old pickup they'd borrowed from somewhere. They left without even

August. During the whole time, Larry hardly said a word to me when he came to pick up my mother. A few times, he gave me a quick handshake, but only when Aunt Fay was watching.

"I'm *not* rushing," Mom replied. "Larry thinks it's the right time, and I think it'll be good for me and Ben to be on our own instead of depending on you for everything. Besides, Larry's already found us a place. We're moving in two weeks."

Two weeks. I couldn't believe it. I didn't want to go anywhere. I liked living with Aunt Fay, reading her books and eating stacks of buttery pancakes after church on Sundays with the sun shining right into her living room. It was better than any place Mom and I ever lived in, but I couldn't say that. I couldn't even speak, I was so upset.

Aunt Fay wasn't happy either. She kept shaking her head like she did whenever something bad happened in our neighborhood. I knew why.

Our neighbor Jackie knew Larry from high school. I'd overheard her telling Aunt Fay about him one night back in July. She said people used to call Larry "The Big Hurt" for all the

"Larry and I are getting married," my mom announced.

We were at the small kitchen table in my Aunt Fay's apartment. My aunt was across from me grading her students' homework. She's an eighth grade teacher who also taught summer school. I was eating pancakes and almost choked when I heard the news.

"*What?!*" Aunt Fay asked, dropping her pen. "You've only been seeing him for a few months. If things are still good after a year or so, *then* marry him. Right now seems too soon, Geneva. You're not pregnant, so why are you rushing?"

Aunt Fay was right. It was too fast.

Larry Taylor and Mom started seeing each other May of my freshman year at Lincoln High School. Now it was only

Find out what happens next at

BLUFORD HIGH

Search for Safety

There is no escape for Ben McKee. For weeks, he's covered the bruises on his body. He's even lied to his teachers and new friends at Bluford High School. But the trouble in Ben's house isn't going away. And if he doesn't act soon, it could swallow him and his mother forever.

Turn the page for a special sneak preview. . . .

Shattered

PAUL LANGAN

Series Editor: Paul Langan

SCHOLASTIC INC.
New York Toronto London Auckland
Sydney Mexico City New Delhi Hong Kong

ISBN 978-0-545-45019-5

Copyright © 2007 by Townsend Press, Inc.
All rights reserved. Published by Scholastic Inc.,
557 Broadway, New York, NY 10012, by arrangement
with Townsend Press, Inc. SCHOLASTIC and associated logos
are trademarks and/or registered trademarks of Scholastic Inc.

12 11 10 9 8 7 6 5 4 3 2 1   12 13 14 15 16 17/0

Printed in the U.S.A.   23

First Scholastic printing, January 2012

Chapter 1

"Girl, where you at?"

Darcy Wills winced at the voice blasting through her new cell phone. It was her best friend, Tarah Carson, and she sounded angry.

"C'mon, Darce. You're late," Tarah scolded.

Darcy knew Tarah was right even before she looked at her watch. She should have left the house ten minutes ago. Instead she was staring at her reflection in the bathroom mirror, hoping Hakeem Randall wouldn't notice the guilt in her eyes or the worry that haunted her face. So much had changed in the few months since they'd broken up. *Too much*, Darcy thought.

"I'm sorry, Tarah. It's just that—"

"Tell her I'm starvin'," yelled Cooper

1

Hodden, Tarah's boyfriend, in the background. "Tell her if she don't get here soon, I'ma start eatin' without her."

His voice was so loud Darcy held the cell phone away from her ear. It sounded like he and Tarah were in the hallway, not several blocks away at Niko's Pizza.

"Stop talkin' nonsense, Coop," Tarah replied. "We ain't eatin' nothin' till she gets here."

"C'mon, Tar! Why you gotsta be that way?" Cooper complained. "Don't ya hear my stomach growlin'?"

"Hold on one second, girl," Tarah said.

Darcy listened as Tarah started hollering at Cooper. She put the phone down to inspect her face again, paying special attention to a tiny pimple just above her right eyebrow.

Why does it have to be there now, she thought, dabbing it with a bit of cover-up. She'd already covered it once, but she wanted to make sure it was invisible to Hakeem.

It wasn't the only thing she hoped to hide.

"Hello? You still there?" Tarah asked.

Darcy quickly grabbed the phone off the bathroom counter.

"Yeah, I'm leavin' right now," she

replied. A jolt of nervous energy raced down her back, making her stomach tremble. An hour of trying on different outfits, messing with her hair, and putting on makeup hadn't calmed her nerves. She still felt tense about seeing Hakeem again, especially after what happened over the summer.

"*You mean you didn't even leave yet?*" Tarah shouted. Darcy held the phone away from her ear again, but there was no escaping her friend's yelling. "We was supposed to meet fifteen minutes ago!"

"I know. I'm sorry, but things were busy at Scoops, and my manager made me stay late," Darcy lied, annoyed at herself for being dishonest with her best friend.

It was true the ice cream store had a busy day. Though it was early September, the weather was as hot as mid-July, and Scoops had been crammed with people buying ice cream. But Darcy's manager, Tamika Ardis, never asked her to stay late. Instead, she sent Darcy home early after she argued with a customer. Darcy had been rushing to prepare two milkshakes when she heard someone call out to her.

"Where's the rest of my change?"

Darcy turned to face a large woman with a tight weave. Two kids huddled close to the woman's legs, holding sticky, half-eaten ice cream cones that dripped onto the floor. Darcy had served them just a few minutes earlier.

"I already gave it to you, ma'am," Darcy replied.

"You better check your register or learn to count or somethin' 'cause I gave you a $20 bill. You just shortchanged me $10," the woman snapped, her free hand resting on her hips.

Darcy took a deep breath. All summer, she'd dealt with customers who treated her and her coworker Haley like trash. Usually Darcy just smiled and ignored it when people were mean, but today she didn't have any patience.

"You don't need to be rude, ma'am," Darcy replied. The words had slipped out so fast Darcy was stunned. So was Haley, who at that moment dropped a small chocolate sundae onto her cash register.

"*Excuse me?*" the woman said, nudging aside the person who'd been at the head of the line. "Girl, you best check that register and yo' mouth and give me

my change, or I'ma make a scene up in here."

"Ma'am, let me finish with this customer first, and I'll help you," Darcy replied, still holding the milkshakes in her hands.

"No, you're gonna help me *now*. I waited in line once. I ain't waitin' again."

Darcy felt her temper building. She couldn't tell the customer off; that would only get her fired. And she couldn't admit she was too stressed to focus on her work. That would only make the woman angrier. For several long seconds, Darcy didn't know what to say. Her mind had gone blank.

"It's okay, ma'am. I can help you," Tamika cut in just in time. "Let's check the register."

Darcy watched as her manager unlocked the cash drawer. She was sure she hadn't miscounted. In her months on the job, she had made plenty of mistakes, but never with money. At Scoops and at Bluford High where she was about to start her junior year, numbers were always something Darcy was good at.

But inside the cash drawer, Tamika found a $20 bill sitting in the $10 slot. Darcy knew instantly she had made a

mistake, and the customer had been right. Darcy felt her cheeks burn with embarrassment.

"I'm so sorry, ma'am," Darcy said as Tamika handed over the money.

"Mmm hmm." The woman scowled and walked out with her children.

"What's wrong with you, Darcy? I've never seen you act that way, and I never want to see it again," Tamika warned as soon as the store emptied out. "I can't afford to upset customers. It's hard enough to stay in business around here as it is."

"I'm sorry. I just got a lot on my mind."

"I hope it's not serious, Darcy. I need you around here. I wish I had two of you."

"No, it's not. It's just . . ." Darcy paused, trying to decide how honest she should be. Tamika recently offered to increase her hours. Darcy didn't want her to change her mind.

"It's her boyfriend, I mean *ex-boyfriend*," cut in Haley, her blond pony-tail poking through the back of her green Scoops visor.

Darcy's jaw dropped. Haley had promised never to tell anyone what they

discussed at work, especially not Tamika.

"He's been in Detroit for months, and tonight she's gonna see him for the first time since he got back. She doesn't want to admit it, but she's really excited," Haley continued with a smile. "And kinda nervous too."

"*Haley, shut your mouth!*" Darcy snapped, embarrassed to hear her personal life being discussed with her boss. "That was between you and me."

"Relax, Darcy. I'm just telling her why you're so out of it. It's not like she hasn't noticed. You're on another planet today," Haley explained.

"I'm *not* out of it. I just miscounted some change, that's all. Not like *you* never made a mistake, Haley."

"Don't even go there, Darce. This isn't about me, and you know it."

Darcy knew Haley was right. All day, she kept forgetting customers' orders. It got so bad she started writing everything down like her first week on the job. Even when she tried to listen to people, all Darcy could hear were the questions racing through her mind.

Should I tell Hakeem about what happened to me this summer?

If I tell him the truth, will he blame me

7

or think I'm a bad person?

Will we ever get back together?

"Haley's right," Tamika said, putting a hand on Darcy's shoulder.

"But—"

"It's okay, Darcy. I know you're a great worker, but today you're having a bad day. Lord knows I've had my share. When I think about it, almost all of them have to do with men," Tamika said with a knowing smile. "Why don't you take the rest of the afternoon off. Haley and I can handle things until closing."

"Are you serious?" Darcy asked. It felt wrong to have everyone know her business, but she needed the break to clear her head and get ready.

"Yeah, go and have fun. Not too much fun, though," Tamika said.

"And whatever you do, be sure someone else counts your change tonight," Haley teased.

Darcy left Scoops in a daze. It was true Hakeem distracted her from work, but there were other things tugging at her too. The summer had been like the earthquakes that sometimes cracked sidewalks and shattered windows in her neighborhood. Only this time, the quake centered on Darcy's house. She still felt

8

aftershocks.

Grandma's quiet death in the bedroom next to Darcy's.

Her parents' announcement that they were having a baby.

Her old friend Brisana's pregnancy scare.

Deeper still was what happened one afternoon just after she and Hakeem broke up. That's when Brian Mason came around with his shiny red Toyota, his smooth voice and wide, dark shoulders. He was nineteen. Darcy babysat for his sister, Liselle. Just thinking of Brian made Darcy nauseous.

Should I tell Hakeem what happened?

For a while, it seemed like a question she wouldn't have to answer. The day Hakeem left, Darcy was sure she'd never see him again. His father was battling cancer, and his family was broke from medical bills. Their only choice was to move in with relatives in faraway Detroit. Hakeem and Darcy split up just before they left.

The loss crushed Darcy. Her boyfriend for most of their sophomore year, Hakeem had also been one of her closest friends at Bluford. He had stood by her no matter what drama was happening in

her life, and there had been plenty, especially since her father returned after abandoning the family for five years. When they said goodbye for the last time, they promised to stay in touch and to always be honest with each other.

Darcy hadn't kept that promise.

For months, she ignored the voice in her head, the one that made her feel guilty whenever she stared at Hakeem's picture collecting dust in her room.

Then a miracle happened. Hakeem's father's health improved, and he allowed his son to live with Cooper and return to Bluford High. Darcy was thrilled beyond words at the news, but her past with Brian still haunted her.

There was no way she could tell Hakeem what happened. No way she could admit she'd gone to Brian's apartment to be alone with him. No way she could say Brian soothed the ache she felt when Hakeem left. And there was something else she couldn't confess to Hakeem.

Brian had gone too far. They had been on his couch kissing, and everything was okay until he tried to work his hands under her shirt.

"*Relax*," he said when she grabbed

his hand.

Then she felt him tugging at her clothes again. His scratchy palm slid against the sensitive skin of her stomach. This time, she told him point-blank to stop. She even tried to push him away. He got angry.

"You're acting like a baby!" he yelled. She tried to get off the couch, but he was too strong. Within seconds, he had her pinned. Sometimes she could still feel how he held her down, his hands gripping her like chains, his strong body pressing against hers. For a frightening instant, she realized she couldn't escape him.

But her father arrived and stopped Brian in his tracks.

"If you ever mess with my daughter again, it will be the last mistake you make!" Dad yelled with a wild rage in his eyes, slamming Brian against a wall. Brian moved out a few days later, but the damage was done.

For weeks afterward, Darcy relived the attack in nightmares. In them, Brian was even more violent, and Dad never arrived to save her. The dreams got so severe she couldn't sleep. Then she started having panic attacks. Things got

so bad Darcy told her parents and Tarah about her problem. She even met for weeks with a counselor at the community center where Tarah worked. Over time, the nightmares and panic attacks faded. But the scars were still there.

Darcy felt them gnawing at her as she left Scoops. Felt them as she prepared to meet Hakeem for the first time since he returned. Felt them even now as she spoke with Tarah on her cell phone.

"Look, Darce, are you comin' out or not?" Tarah asked, shattering her thoughts.

Darcy sighed and put her makeup away.

"I'll be there, Tar'," she said. "Ten minutes. I promise."

"If you're not, we're comin' over there and draggin' you out," Tarah warned.

"I'll be there," Darcy repeated, smoothing out her shirt one last time and inspecting the way her body filled her jeans. "I'm leaving right now."

Tarah hung up, and Darcy headed out the door, rushing toward Niko's.

Should I tell Hakeem what happened?

She still didn't know the answer.

Chapter 2

Darcy spotted everyone sitting at the usual table in the back corner of Niko's. The restaurant looked the same as always, crowded with Bluford students and other young people eating, talking, and laughing loudly.

But to Darcy, Niko's felt different since Hakeem left—smaller, though she knew it couldn't be.

"There she is!" shouted Cooper as soon as she neared the table. "Let's eat!"

"Coop, would you at least let her sit down first?" Tarah scolded.

"Sorry, y'all," Cooper said. "But I worked all day and didn't have no lunch break. If I don't get some pepperoni pizza right now, I'ma eat Darcy's chair. Then she won't have a place to sit."

"Coop!" Tarah yelled, slapping him

13

playfully in the chest.

"It's all right. I'm sorry I kept you all waiting. It's just been one of those days," Darcy said, glancing at Tarah and then Hakeem.

He stood up immediately in saggy jeans and a loose white T-shirt. Even in those clothes, Darcy could see he'd grown over the summer, not taller, but wider and more muscular. And he seemed older, too, and more handsome. For a split second, she could hear the voice in her head confessing everything to him.

While you were gone, I started seeing someone else. He tried to hurt me. It was a mistake. Please don't hate me. I still want us to get back together like old times.

But as she looked into his eyes, her mouth felt locked tight, as if an invisible hand gripped her face.

"Hi, Hakeem," she said, forcing herself to speak. She could barely manage a smile she was so tense.

Hakeem gave her a quick, firm hug, patting her back twice like she was his aunt. The touch made Darcy cringe inside. It was nothing like the embraces they'd shared only months ago.

"Good to s-s-see you, Darce," he said, looking at her quickly and turning away. Darcy was surprised to hear his stutter. It was a problem that surfaced when he was nervous or stressed. Normally it happened when he talked to adults, not with her.

"You too," she replied, wondering if her touch felt as uncomfortable as his.

Darcy felt Tarah watching them, trying to figure out what was wrong. Darcy wanted to talk to her alone but didn't know how to ask without seeming rude. Instead, she sat down at the table. Several seconds passed without a word. It felt like hours to Darcy.

"So can we eat?" Cooper blurted out, his voice shattering the heavy silence that gathered over their table like fog.

"Yeah, I been dreaming about Niko's pizza for months," Hakeem said, turning to Cooper and sitting down. "What are we waiting for?"

"Amen!" Coop shouted, jumping up to place the order.

For a second, the table got quiet again, and Darcy wondered what she could say that would seem natural. Looking at Hakeem, she could swear he felt just as awkward.

15

Was he holding something back too? she wondered.

"So can y'all believe it?" Tarah asked suddenly, her voice a bit forced. "We're juniors. I can't believe it myself. Where'd the time go?"

Hakeem sighed and rubbed his forehead.

Darcy squirmed in her seat, grateful to see Cooper return to the table. She knew Tarah was trying to get them to talk, but her questions only made things more tense. Tarah's long stares didn't help either. Darcy felt like she was on one of those reality TV shows her younger sister Jamee watched where people pretended to act normal even though five cameras were in their faces.

"I hear what you sayin', girl," Cooper cut in. "Seems like yesterday Darcy was just a know-it-all in Ms. Reed's class who did nothin' but hit the books. Now we know she can hang, and we all tight."

"Thanks a lot, Coop," Darcy replied, remembering how at the beginning of last year, she and Tarah were nearly enemies. It was all ancient history.

"Seems like yesterday you had a big mouth and no sense. But nothin's changed, Coop, 'cause you actin' that

16

way right now," Tarah cut back, glaring at him.

"That's cold," he replied, acting hurt.

"But it's true," Tarah shot back.

"I know what Coop's trying to s-s-say," Hakeem spoke up suddenly. "Look how much we all changed in just one year. If Coop's mom didn't let me stay at his crib, I wouldn't even be here. Who knows where we'll be a year from now."

"Man, Detroit sure made you serious, bro," Cooper said.

"It *is* serious, Coop. When my dad got sick, I went from worrying about grades to wondering whether he'd even make it. I saw things change just like that." He snapped his fingers to make his point.

"Once you go through that, life ain't the same. You start thinking differently about everything. Maybe some things aren't what you thought they were. I don't mean to sound depressing, but the truth is you don't know what's gonna happen. We might not be here next week, forget about next year," Hakeem continued, looking at each person at the table as he spoke. There was a depth in his eyes that Darcy didn't remember. The summer had changed him too, no

doubt about it.

"I know what you mean," Darcy replied. "I feel the same way. With Grandma passing away and the baby coming and . . ." She paused. She knew her thoughts were drifting toward Brian. She wasn't about to go there, not with everyone staring at her. Not with the strange, new Hakeem across from her. "You just change, you know. Some things don't seem as important as they used to."

Darcy felt a wave of sadness as she spoke. Maybe what they were really saying was that things were over between them. The months apart had destroyed what little remained of their friendship, dried it up like a plant left in the sun too long without water. Their old relationship was finally dead.

Tarah leaned forward, shaking her head as if what she heard bothered her.

"I hear what y'all are sayin', and I know you're bein' real, but you're forgettin' somethin'. Friends and family ain't like clothes that go out of style. You don't just drop your people." Tarah paused and looked at Darcy, then back at Hakeem. "When stuff happens, which it always does, you work through it.

That don't mean it's easy. I'd be lyin' if I said that. But it's what you gotta do when somethin's important."

Darcy shifted uncomfortably in her chair. She noticed Hakeem was playing with a straw, his eyes aimed down at the table, not at her.

"It's kinda like pizza," Cooper said.

Tarah rolled her eyes and shook her head in frustration.

"Yo, you *really* need to eat something, Coop," Hakeem added, smiling slightly.

"I'm serious. Check this out. Say you find something you really like—like pepperoni pizza. Why change anything if it's that good? If you did, you'd throw away something special. Once y'all try a slice, you'll see what I mean. Some things don't need to change." Cooper's eyes were fixed on Hakeem. Tarah's were too.

Hakeem grunted and tossed his straw aside. Darcy took a sip of water.

"Two pizzas?" the waiter interrupted, carrying two large trays.

"Yeah, you can put that one right in front of me," Cooper instructed.

Darcy smiled as Cooper quickly grabbed two slices, wincing as a glob of hot cheese landed on his wrist. Across

19

from him, she noticed Hakeem's face. For several seconds, he didn't budge even though the pizza was right in front of him.

What's wrong with him? Darcy wondered. Though he was sitting next to her, Hakeem still seemed miles away.

Does he know I'm hiding something? Is that why he's so different? Or is it something else?

"You all right, Darce?" Tarah asked.

"Huh?" Darcy said. She noticed Cooper and Hakeem weren't at the table. They were standing in line at the cash register.

"What's botherin' you, girl? You hardly said anything tonight, and you only ate one slice of pizza. You feelin' okay?"

Darcy realized she'd been so distracted she didn't even see Cooper and Hakeem get up. She must have zoned out for at least a few minutes. "I'm fine, Tarah. I just got a lot on my mind, that's all," Darcy explained.

In line at the register, Cooper and Hakeem spoke quietly to each other. Darcy noticed Cooper did most of the talking.

"Well, spit it out, girl. You look more like you just said goodbye to Hakeem, not hello," Tarah said.

"I know, Tar. I'm sorry, it's just . . . " Darcy paused, lowering her voice so no one but Tarah could hear. "It's me and Hakeem. You saw how weird we were tonight. I never thought I'd say it, but I think it's finally over," she admitted. There was something sad and final in the word *over*. It seemed to echo in the air as she said it.

"C'mon, Darce! Hakeem just got back. Give him some time, girl. You both just need to get used to each other again. And you two need to talk and deal with what happened this summer so you can move on, you know. Just don't worry," Tarah said, rubbing her back.

Darcy wanted the words to be true, but she didn't believe them, not with what she'd just heard.

"You know what else?" she added, lowering her voice further so it was barely louder than a whisper. "I keep thinking about what happened with Brian. How am I ever gonna tell Hakeem about that? He'd never understand. He'd hate me."

Tarah sighed and rubbed Darcy's back without saying a word. Usually,

she had a quick answer for everything. The fact that Tarah took so long to respond made Darcy feel even worse. It was like having a disease the doctor could not cure. Tarah might as well have come out and said, *"Yep, you're right, girl. You screwed up big-time, and ain't nothin' gonna fix it. Sorry."*

"Give it time, girl," Tarah said finally. "When you're ready, tell him what you need to tell him. If he's the person I think he is, he'll handle it just right. If not, you're better off without him." She stopped to eat a piece of hardened cheese she'd picked off the tray in front of her. "Like I said, both of you need to talk and sort things out. You don't need to rush anything. But I'm bein' straight up with you about this. I think you two can work everything out."

"Are you serious, Tarah? You really think so? You're not just saying that?" Darcy stared into Tarah's eyes, searching for a reason to believe her.

While Tarah didn't look away, she paused just a bit. Maybe no one else would have noticed it, but Darcy did.

"You know it, girl."

The two were quiet for a minute as Darcy replayed Tarah's words over and

over again in her mind. The way she'd paused didn't sound right. Like an off-key voice in a choir. And there was something strange in Tarah's advice too.

"*You two need to deal with what happened this summer,*" she had said. "*Both of you need to sort things out.*" Those words: *you two. Both of you.* What did they mean? Did Tarah know more than she was saying?

Darcy was about to ask when Hakeem and Cooper returned.

"Well, we should get back. First day of school is tomorrow," Hakeem said. "I still got some unpacking to do."

First day of school. The words seemed like a cruel joke, but they were true. Tomorrow would pile classes and homework on top of everything else swirling in Darcy's head. But no matter what her classes would bring, Darcy knew one question she needed an answer to first.

What happened to Hakeem this summer?

Chapter 3

Darcy rushed home to call Tarah. She'd just crossed the street onto her block when she heard people arguing. The street was mostly empty, so Darcy figured one of her elderly neighbors was watching TV with the volume turned way up. But as she got closer to her doorstep, Darcy realized the sound was coming from inside her house.

"Forget about it, Mattie!" Dad yelled as Darcy opened the door. His voice boomed from the kitchen. "You are *not* going to do that. I won't allow it. End of story."

Darcy was shocked. Dad had never spoken to her mother that way. She rushed in to see what was happening.

"You don't get to tell me what I can and can't do, Carl!" Mom hollered back. She was standing in the middle of the

kitchen, her arms crossed over her chest. She was still wearing the ID badge from the hospital where she worked as an emergency-room nurse. Dad was at the sink washing dishes. Both of them looked exhausted and upset. Neither seemed to notice Darcy standing in the hallway.

"I do when it comes to the health of my child," Dad replied. "Stop being so stubborn, Mattie!"

"Don't talk to me in that tone of voice. You got no right." Mom fumed, her jaw jutting out sharply with anger.

Darcy froze, afraid to get between them while they were fighting. Just then, Jamee came out of her bedroom and joined her in the hallway. Jamee gaped as if she couldn't believe what she was seeing.

"I'm that baby's father, Mattie. That's all the right I need," Dad challenged.

For weeks, Darcy had sensed the tension building in the house. The clues were everywhere, in the way her mother sighed whenever anyone talked about money, in the desperate way her father searched the newspaper for job listings, in the long walks he took alone in the evenings.

It started when his hours were cut at the fancy clothing store where he worked as a salesperson. Since then, her mother and father were always tense. Mom walked around with dark, baggy circles under her eyes. Dad talked less and seemed moody, always shuffling papers and rushing off to go somewhere. About the only thing that seemed to cheer them up was when they talked about the baby, but even the joy of that news had faded recently.

Sometimes, late at night, Darcy would listen to them exchanging words with each other. She knew they'd been trying to hide their problems from her and Jamee, but it wasn't working. Darcy figured a major fight was coming, but she never imagined it would be this loud and hurtful, or that it would explode like a bomb the night before the first day of school.

"You lost *that* right when you walked out on us, Carl! You haven't earned it back yet," Mom lashed back. "I worked fifty to sixty hours a week for the first few years after you left us for that other woman. I can do it again if I have to."

Dad tipped forward as if he'd been kicked in the stomach.

Crash!

The large plate in his hand fell to the kitchen floor and shattered.

Darcy's jaw dropped. She looked at Jamee, who had tears in her eyes. She grabbed her hand and fought the urge to jump in between her parents. It was like watching a horrible accident happen right in front of her eyes.

Dad slammed his fists on the counter and stepped away from the sink, crunching pieces of the broken plate under his feet. His face was twisted with pain, an image out of a nightmare.

Darcy knew Mom's words hurt. Dad's biggest regret was that he'd started drinking and walked out on his family, leaving them for five long years. Since he'd returned last fall, he'd done nothing but apologize and try to undo the damage he caused.

"Why do you *always* have to go there, Mattie?" her father asked. His normally strong voice shook with emotion, a terrible sad sound that made Darcy want to cover her ears. "That was years ago, and it has nothing to do with us right now. We're both different people. I apologized a thousand times, but you just won't let it go."

"Because whenever I start to depend on you, I remember what happened the last time I did. I'm sorry, but this ain't easy for me, Carl. And your plan—to be a nighttime cab driver—is not gonna solve our problems."

"It's only until I find something better, Mattie," Dad explained. "Besides, I know this city well enough to stay out of the bad areas. And I can handle myself. Remember, I did some boxing in the Army."

"No, it's still not safe, Carl," Mom insisted. "I've seen too many cabbies in the ER. With a baby on the way, you've got to think about the bigger picture. We can't afford to have something happen to you."

"Mattie, I *am* thinking about the bigger picture. I'm a black man in this city in my forties without a college degree. Right now, I've gotta take whatever I can get. When I find something better, I'll move on. But I'm not gonna sit still and let you work sixty hours a week, especially when you're carrying our baby. Don't ask me to let that happen, 'cause I can't do it."

Dad stared at her as he spoke. Mom grabbed a broom and dustpan from the

tiny kitchen closet. Darcy admired what her father was saying. She knew Mom shouldn't work any more hours in the hospital than she had to. Even before she was pregnant, she would come home tired. But lately she seemed more weary than ever. Dad was just trying to help out. He was taking the job for the family, not himself.

"Well you should have thought about that before," Mom snapped. "I told you I wasn't ready to do this again, and you said not to worry. And now look at us. We got all these new bills for this house *you* wanted. We got a child on the way, and the only job you can find is one that has you drivin' in the 'hood at two in the morning! Now you see why I'm upset. You asked me to trust you, and look what *you* did. You got us into trouble again, Carl. I shoulda known better than to listen to you!"

"That's not fair, Mattie."

"You want to know what's not fair, Carl? That I dealt with your mistakes alone for five long years, and now you're asking me to do it again," she yelled, her words like sharp knives.

Dad shook his head. "I don't know why I even bother tryin' to talk to you

29

sometimes," he said, drying his hands on his pants. He stepped over the mess on the kitchen floor and practically ran into Darcy and Jamee. He stared at them, sighed, and then grabbed his keys.

"Where are you going?" Mom asked as he put on his old baseball cap and jacket.

Without a word, Dad walked out, slamming the door behind him.

Mom raced past Darcy and Jamee to the doorway.

"So that's it? You just gonna walk out again? You haven't changed one bit, Carl!" Mom yelled so loud the whole block could hear her voice. "*Not one bit!*"

Darcy wanted to follow him—anything to get away from the house, which suddenly felt more like a prison than a home.

"What are you two looking at?" Mom said, turning to them like the argument was their fault. Darcy knew it wasn't the time to talk to her mother, not with the veins in her forehead bulging with anger, not with the tears in her eyes.

"C'mon, Jamee," Darcy said, tugging her sister by her sleeve.

"No, Darcy," Jamee refused, shrugging Darcy off and turning to Mom. "I'm

not going anywhere. You're not fair, Mom. He's only tryin' to help. You can't work those hours anymore. It's not good for the baby. And if you keep treatin' Dad like that, he's gonna run away again."

"*Jamee!*" Darcy yelled. She couldn't believe her ears. Nothing had hurt Mom more than when Dad left with another woman. Sometimes Darcy still had flashbacks to her mother crying like a baby in Grandma's arms. It was the saddest sound she'd ever heard. Now Jamee was practically blaming Mom for what happened. It was the most hurtful thing she could have said.

In one swift move, Mom stepped forward and swung her arm with her hand outstretched.

Slap!

Mom's palm struck Jamee's cheek, knocking her back into a wall. Darcy winced at the cracking sound, which seemed to boom through the air like a gunshot.

Her mother hadn't hit either of them in years. But the look in her angry, unblinking eyes said she might do it again.

Jamee's mouth was wide open with shock. She rubbed her face where

Mom's hand struck her. Darcy moved in between them. She had to do something to stop things from getting worse.

"Don't, Mom! Jamee didn't mean it that way," Darcy said as Mom moved closer.

"Don't you *ever* talk to me like that again! You hear me!" Mom screamed, pointing at Jamee. Darcy stood between them, bracing herself.

"Mom, please—"

"And you stay out of this too, Darcy. This is between your father and me."

"What's your problem? We're in this family too," Jamee yelled, still rubbing her cheek. Darcy could hear the hurt and outrage in her voice.

"Jamee, just shut up!" Darcy said, grabbing Jamee's shoulders to calm her.

"Don't touch me!" Jamee yelled, shoving her hands aside.

Mom stormed down the hallway into her bedroom. She slammed the door behind her, knocking an old picture of Grandma to the floor. Jamee rushed the opposite way, out the front door.

Darcy stood in the suddenly quiet hallway alone.

It was as if a bomb had exploded, splitting the house into hundreds of

pieces, leaving everyone too wounded to speak.

Darcy went out looking for Jamee ten minutes later.

She found her sitting on the front step of their house. It was dark, but Jamee's face was lit by the glow of a cigarette that dangled from her mouth. Supposedly she'd given up smoking last year after she dumped her abusive boyfriend, Bobby Wallace.

"Leave me alone," Jamee said coldly. "And don't lecture me about smoking. I know it's no good for me. Right now, I really don't care."

Darcy sat down next to her without a word. Her foot knocked over a beer bottle left on the sidewalk in front of their house. It rolled loudly into the dark. Even in the shadows, Darcy could see Jamee's eyes were swollen, her face wet with tears.

"Would you just go back inside," Jamee growled. "I don't need you out here. I don't need anybody."

Darcy put her hand on her sister's back. At first Jamee squirmed away, but then she stopped moving and let Darcy's arm rest on her shoulder.

"What's happening to us, Darce?" Jamee asked.

"It's just a fight, that's all. You always accuse me of worrying too much. Look at you now," Darcy said, wishing her words were more helpful, more convincing. But after the day she had, it was all she could think of. "They'll be okay. We'll be okay. I promise."

Jamee sniffled and wiped her eyes. "I miss Grandma," she said.

"Me too, Jamee," Darcy said, feeling the words deep in her chest. Grandma had always been the refuge they could go to, no matter what happened. Her absence left a gaping hole in Darcy's heart, one that seemed wider than ever. "Me too."

Jamee quietly took the cigarette from her mouth and crushed it into the ground. For several minutes, they didn't say anything.

"What if he leaves us again?" she asked.

It was a question Darcy asked herself many times since Dad had returned. For a while, she hadn't allowed herself to believe he was back. That way she could never be hurt again. But after all the helpful things he did over the past year,

she gradually began to believe in him. And with the house, the new baby, and Grandma gone, she could not imagine him ever leaving.

But what happened tonight never happened before. A line had been crossed. What once seemed rock solid now felt like it had deep cracks. Like it could all come crashing down one day soon, a landslide that would claim her family as its victims.

"He won't," Darcy said, trying to convince herself as much as her sister. "He wouldn't do that again."

It was well past midnight when Darcy finally crawled into bed to sleep. In the kitchen, the shattered plate still littered the floor.

And her father hadn't come home.

Chapter 4

Darcy woke up with the worst headache.

It was 6:45 when she slammed the snooze button of her blaring alarm clock, hoping last night's fight was just another bad dream and summer break wasn't over.

But when she crawled out of bed, Darcy discovered her mother in the kitchen sweeping pieces of the broken plate into a dustpan. It was all too real.

"Dad's not back yet?" she asked.

"*No*," Mom said sternly, dumping the dustpan into the trash. She looked like she hadn't slept at all. Darcy could tell from her puffy, swollen eyes that she'd been crying.

"Where is he?"

"How should I know?" Mom snapped.

"No phone call. No nothing. I don't know what that man's doing."

Darcy cringed inside. She knew what those words sounded like, how they opened up old wounds. She was sure Dad was coming back, that he'd just gotten really upset from her mother's harsh words. What Mom said wasn't fair, but that didn't give Dad the right to just walk out without a word. Not with the painful memories of the past still haunting them all, especially not with Mom being pregnant.

"I'm sure he's comin' back—"

"I don't want to hear it. I am so mad at him right now, I can't even think straight," her mother warned.

Darcy wished she could do something to calm her. Anything. "Mom, I saved some money working at Scoops. If you need it, you and Dad can have it. And I can work more hours if it helps. Tamika even asked if I—"

"No," Mom said. "That's *your* money. I won't have you payin' for our mess. If I gotta work overtime to keep a roof over our head, that's what I'll do."

"But what about the baby, Mom? You can't do what you used—"

"Now don't *you* start with me. I can

and I will," Mom said. Her words were firm, but there was something hollow in the way she said them. Darcy also noticed she swept the floor too forcefully, spreading the shards of the broken plate instead of sweeping them up.

"Here, let me help you, Mom," Darcy said, reaching for the broom.

"The best way you can help me right now is to leave me alone," her mother grumbled.

"But Mom—"

"Just go, Darcy. Get ready for school," Mom insisted. "I'll take care of this."

Darcy forced herself out of the kitchen, pretending not to see the tears in her mother's tired eyes.

Darcy heard the front door open just as she finished getting dressed. She was sure Dad had finally come home, but when she walked into the living room, she didn't find her father. Instead, she saw Jamee rushing down the street. Darcy shook her head in frustration. Jamee had left for school without her.

Outside, the sun hung bright and golden over the neighborhood, making Darcy squint as she walked out the

door. Though it was early, she could already feel the heat building and knew it was going to be another summery day. But the sunlight only mocked her gloomy mood.

Clusters of students headed quietly down the street toward Bluford High School. Many of them looked young and scared as they slowly passed Niko's, the Golden Grill Restaurant, and the Korean grocery store.

"Have a good day, Harold," said an old woman from the third floor window of a nearby apartment building. She had a friendly, round face, and she waved gently to a thick-bodied boy standing on the sidewalk in front of Darcy.

"Thanks, Grandma," he replied somberly. He spoke like he was heading to a funeral, not his first day of high school. He looked a bit embarrassed when he saw Darcy pass by.

Darcy smiled, remembering how nervous she'd been on her first day at Bluford. She was so scared she almost got sick to her stomach. Mom had to work that day, and Dad was long gone, so Grandma decided to walk her to the front door of the school to make her feel better.

"Don't you worry, Angelcake. You're gonna shine at this school. I know it. One day, you'll look back at this moment, smile, and wonder where all the time went. You mark my words."

Two years had passed since that day, and already Darcy knew Grandma was right. If only she could still talk to her. Tell her about the new baby, about the troubles at home with Dad. Get her advice about Hakeem.

Hakeem. In all the drama at home, Darcy had almost forgotten about the awkward dinner at Niko's. She had to talk to Tarah right away and find out what was wrong with him.

Up ahead on the other side of the street, Darcy spotted a couple her age holding hands and laughing. She couldn't help but stare at them as they strolled together in the morning sun. Seeing them made Darcy feel even more miserable.

See what you lost, they seemed to say.

Darcy walked faster just so she wouldn't have to look at them. After a few minutes, she reached the supermarket parking lot that bordered Bluford and glimpsed the main steps leading to the

school's front doors. Three security guards in blue uniforms stood with Ms. Spencer, the school principal, at the top of the steps. They were checking students with metal detectors as they entered. Next to the school, Darcy could see the blue and yellow sign hanging behind the bleachers of the football field.

Welcome to Bluford High School
Home of the Buccaneers

Even though she'd been there two years, Darcy still felt her stomach jump at the sight of the school. Taking a deep breath, she climbed the main steps to begin her junior year.

The hallway inside was crowded with students rushing in all directions. Many of them were holding schedules and looking at room numbers trying to figure out where they were going.

Freshmen, Darcy thought to herself.

Ahead of her, Darcy spotted Jamee standing with Amberlynn Bailey and Cindy Gibson. The two girls had been her sister's closest friends since elementary school. Each had an arm around Jamee, who wiped her eyes several times.

Though she couldn't hear them,

Darcy knew exactly what they were talking about: last night. She passed them, glad to see Jamee had friends to support her, though she suddenly felt alone in the crowded hallway. She wondered where Tarah, Hakeem, and Cooper were.

"There you are! Oh my God, Darcy. We need to talk," said a voice, snapping Darcy from her thoughts.

Darcy turned to see Brisana Meeks. Before last year, Brisana had been her best friend. But everything changed when Darcy started hanging out with Tarah and Cooper, people Brisana hated. Since then, the two had good days and bad days. Darcy hoped this would be a good one.

"What's up, Bris?" Darcy asked, doing her best to smile. She noticed Brisana looked better than ever. She was wearing a sleeveless gray shirt that hugged her body and revealed her curvy figure. Her hair was long and braided with copper highlights, and her cocoa skin was flawless.

What a change from July, Darcy thought, remembering Brisana sobbing in the tiny parking lot behind Scoops. Back then, Brisana thought she was pregnant, and she came to Darcy for help.

Darcy was stunned at the news. For years, Brisana, a fellow honors student, had looked down on people who struggled in school, especially girls who got pregnant.

"That's just dumb. Why would you let something like that happen?" she'd once said about Liselle Mason, a girl they knew who quit school to have a baby.

But then Brisana fell for an older guy who told her he loved her. Darcy knew he was no good. She'd seen him flirting with other girls, but Brisana was blind. Soon she was in over her head, making the same mistakes Liselle made. And because she'd been such a snob, Brisana had few friends to turn to. That's why she came to Darcy. Brisana practically admitted it the morning they went to the clinic and learned the pregnancy scare was a false alarm.

Darcy hoped the episode would change Brisana, make her less likely to judge others. Maybe even help her become friends with Tarah, a girl who was her opposite in many ways. But looking at her now, Darcy saw nothing to indicate she'd changed. If anything, Brisana looked even more her old self, like she was a song on the radio and

someone just turned it louder.

"Look, Darcy, I have something to tell you that you're not gonna want to hear," Brisana said. She had the I-have-a-secret look in her eyes. Darcy had seen it a thousand times before, especially when Brisana was about to gossip. "It's about Hakeem," she added.

"What about him?"

"He's back."

"I know, Brisana. I went out with him last night," Darcy said, sighing with relief. "Why would that be bad news?"

"Listen, Darce. I saw him at the mall Saturday. He was with another girl." She looked into Darcy's eyes as she spoke as if she was trying to see the impact of her words.

Alarms began sounding in Darcy's head. The last time Brisana had given her advice about Hakeem, it was a lie. Brisana had always been jealous of her relationship with Hakeem. Last year she'd even tried to break them up by saying false things about him. But that was so long ago, Darcy was shocked to hear her trying it again.

"C'mon, Bris. I thought we were done all this," she said.

"I'm serious," Brisana insisted. "I

watched them in the food court, Darcy. And from what I could see, they weren't there to eat."

Brisana's story made no sense. Hakeem had barely been back three days. How could he have another girlfriend already? And why was Brisana, the person furthest from Hakeem, the only one who knew about it? There was only one reason: the story was another lie. Brisana wanted to stop them from getting back together. Darcy was sure of it.

"I'm not hearing this," Darcy said, turning and walking down the hallway. Brisana raced to keep up.

"Darcy, I saw him with my own two eyes. I swear."

Darcy wished Brisana's voice sounded less honest. Wished that her stare seemed less sincere.

"Whatever."

"Darcy, I don't know who this girl is. But she looks like she stepped out of a magazine or something. She is *all that*," Brisana said.

"Just stop it, okay! I don't want to hear it," Darcy replied, walking faster. "I really thought we were cool. Since you're lying to me again, I guess I was wrong," Darcy said, acting as if Brisana's words

45

didn't shake her.

"*Lying* to you! Is that what you think I'm doing?" Brisana fumed. "Fine. Be that way. But don't say I didn't tell you. And don't come crying later on just 'cause you were too stubborn to listen."

"If I remember correctly, *you* were the one who came crying to me this summer, so don't try acting like you're all special," Darcy yelled. She knew her words were mean, but at that moment she didn't care.

Brisana gasped as if she'd just been slapped, but Darcy ignored her.

Darcy stormed through the hallway, forcing several freshmen to step aside as she rushed to the closest restroom. Inside, the air was a thick mixture of cleanser, perfume, and a touch of cigarette smoke. Girls hurried in and out, washing their hands, fixing their make-up, inspecting their clothes and hair.

"Oh my God! Tyray looks so *good*," said one girl.

"He does," replied another. "I bet he's a player, though."

Darcy wanted to scream.

She went into a stall, locked it shut, and put her hands over her ears to block out the sounds around her.

But inside her head, voices of doubt were speaking.

And with each second, they grew a bit louder.

Chapter 5

Looks like she stepped out of a maga-
zine . . .
More than friends . . .
Don't say I didn't tell you . . .

Brisana's words echoed in Darcy's
mind as she made her way to Ms. York's
Algebra II class. Even as she sat down at
a desk in the center of the classroom,
Darcy could barely hear what the
teacher was saying over the sound of
Brisana's voice in her head. She was
remembering Hakeem's strange behavior at Niko's when she felt someone tap
her shoulder.

"Yo, pay attention. She's calling you,"
a voice said.

Darcy turned around to see Roylin
Bailey sitting at the desk behind her. He

nodded toward the front of the room.

"Huh?" Darcy asked in confusion. She glanced forward and noticed the whole class staring at her. Ms. York, the pear-shaped woman sitting at the teacher's desk, raised her eyebrows. She held a red pen in her hand, and a black notebook was open in front of her.

"I think you should mark Darcy absent, Ms. York. She's somewhere else right now," Roylin teased. Several people in class laughed.

"Perhaps Mr. Bailey has a point," the teacher said, giving Darcy a stern look.

Darcy immediately realized what happened. She had zoned out again, this time during attendance. She could feel her face burning with embarrassment.

"I'm here . . . sort of," Darcy said, trying to make a joke out of what happened. "Sorry."

"We're glad you're with us, Ms. Wills," Ms. York said, marking her notebook and moving on to the next person.

For the rest of class, Darcy tried to focus on Ms. York's quick review of concepts from geometry and Algebra I. But her mind kept wandering to Brisana's warning and the odd way Hakeem acted the night before. The more she thought

about it, the more Darcy wondered if there might be some truth to what Brisana told her.

Tarah would know. She would ask her during lunch period.

Or just talk to him, Darcy thought to herself. But doing so meant she would have to be honest about Brian. She'd have to admit what happened and what almost happened.

"Is everything okay, Ms. Wills?" a voice suddenly disrupted her thoughts.

"Huh?"

"Class is over. Unless you wish to sit with the freshmen I have next period, I suggest you go to your next class."

"Yes, ma'am," Darcy said, realizing she had done it again. "I just have a lot on my mind," she added, closing her notebook and heading toward the door.

"I can see that," the teacher nodded. "But tomorrow I expect you to actually attend my class, Ms. Wills. Understand?"

"Yes, Ms. York."

Darcy felt the sweat beading on her forehead as she bolted out of the classroom. She had to find out the truth about Hakeem soon.

Before it got her fired from Scoops and flunked out of Bluford.

"Oh my God! You in here too? That's what I'm talkin' 'bout," Tarah cheered and strutted through the doorway of Darcy's third class, chemistry.

Darcy had arrived early and sat in the front row, determined to pay attention. She had no idea Tarah was in the class, but as soon as she saw her, she was relieved. Now she could finally get some answers.

"We gonna have some fun in here, girl. Just like old times back in Ms. Reed's class. You gotsta be my lab partner again," Tarah added, dropping her shiny neon pink backpack down with a loud thud.

Darcy noticed Tarah got her nails done for the first day of school. Each finger ended in a long fake nail coated in colorful designs that sparkled with glittery polish.

"My cousin's friend hooked me up last night after we got back. Ain't they da bomb?" Tarah said, spreading her thick fingers so Darcy could inspect them.

To Darcy, the nails looked like painted claws, not something she would ever wear. Especially not for the lab assignments they might do in chemistry class,

but she wasn't about to say anything. Her mind was on Hakeem.

"They're really nice, Tar," she said quickly, trying her best to sound sincere, though she knew Tarah was too smart to be fooled. "Listen, I need to talk to you about something serious."

"What is it, Darce? Everything okay at home?" Tarah asked, reaching to get something from her backpack.

Darcy paused for a minute. She wasn't ready to go near what happened at home. It was all too much, and Brisana's words were still fresh in her mind. She needed answers about Hakeem. *Now.*

"Go on, girl. Spit it out."

"It's Hakeem. I think he's hiding something from me."

"*Hiding something?*" Tarah repeated, her voice a bit louder than usual.

"Think about it, Tar. The summer's a long time. What if he started seeing someone in Detroit?" Darcy said, watching Tarah's face for clues.

"C'mon, Darce. Why you gotta go there?" Tarah asked as if the idea was crazy. But there was a sad note in her voice, and she avoided looking directly into Darcy's eyes.

Just then, Brisana Meeks walked

into the classroom.

Darcy remained still as Brisana strolled by and grabbed a desk two rows away without even looking in their direction. She knew Brisana had seen her talking to Tarah. Brisana could size up a room better than anyone.

"You would tell me if you knew something, right?" Darcy asked, keeping her voice low.

For a second, Tarah looked like she was in pain. She took a deep breath, glanced quickly at Brisana and then focused on Darcy. "Look, it's like I told you last night. You two need to talk. When you do, things'll be all right. And no matter what happens, y'all will still be friends, right?"

Darcy nearly fell out of her seat.

Friends. It was the "f" word that meant she and Hakeem were completely over. Tarah had never said it before about the two of them. She might as well have just said, *"Give it up, girl. It's over."*

"So it's true then?" Darcy asked, unable to keep her voice down. She could feel eyes watching her, but she didn't care. "He's seeing someone? Come on, Tarah. What's going on?"

Tarah sighed, put both her hands

up, and turned her head away from Darcy. "Look, I'm sorry, girl, but I don't want to be in the middle of a fight between you two. Like I said last night, you just need to talk to Hakeem. He's the one you need to speak to about this, not me."

"*What?*" Darcy gasped. That Tarah said the word *fight* was all the proof she needed. "So all this time you knew something was going on and you hid it from me?"

"I knew this was gonna happen," Tarah said, slumping back in her chair. "Look, I'm sorry, Darcy. I mean it. But from now on, I'm not gonna say nothin' till you talk to Hakeem. I'm outta this."

Darcy couldn't believe her ears. Tarah had practically been lying right to her face. And how long had it been going on? Two days? Two months? Darcy's mind began spinning. She felt like she'd just been kicked in the stomach and slapped in the face at the same time.

"I can't believe you. I trusted you with everything, Tarah. How could you do this? You're supposed to be my friend!" Darcy exclaimed.

"I *am* your friend. But I'm Hakeem's friend too," Tarah replied. "I've known

him since we was five years old. Him and Coop's like brothers, and I hear everything because of that. But it ain't right for me to be tellin' everybody's secrets, especially when the secrets can hurt people."

"That's not right, Tarah. After everything I've told you, you shouldn't be lying to me about Hakeem—"

"Don't get in my face callin' me a liar. Nothin' I said was a lie, and I gave you both the same advice: Talk to each other. Maybe I kept Hakeem's secret. But I also kept yours," Tarah said, sitting up and waving her long-nailed finger at Darcy. "Remember, you haven't told *him* everything either."

Darcy felt her pulse throb and her ears begin to ring. For a second, she wanted to slap Tarah's wide face. Who was she to practically bring up Brian in the middle of a crowded classroom? How dare she act like Darcy's secret was the same as hiding the truth about Hakeem?

"I can't believe you just said that! That's totally different—"

"Why?" Tarah challenged. "You two are supposed to be close, but you keep stuff from him. He keeps it from you. What's different about that?"

"But I trusted you—"

"I didn't break no promises to you," Tarah cut back. "I ain't done nothin' but try to get you two to talk since he got back. Only difference is you want me to tell you his secrets and hide yours. That ain't right. And it ain't fair to expect me to do that."

"Fair?" Darcy yelled back. She couldn't believe how angry she was at Tarah. Since they became friends, she never imagined a time they could yell at each other. But now she couldn't stop.

"I'll tell you what fair is, Tarah. Fair is being straight up with me. Fair is telling me the truth when you say nothing's wrong. Fair is knowing that what happened to me this summer is different than Hakeem kissing some girl at the mall on Saturday. If I saw Cooper doing that, you'd be the first person I'd tell no matter what he said 'cause it's the right thing to do," Darcy hammered back.

"I been tryin' to do the right thing, Darcy. But I couldn't tell you 'cause if I did, you'd lose it, and there'd be no chance of you and Hakeem getting back together," Tarah admitted.

"Well, there's no chance of that now," Darcy said. "We're done."

"Aww snap!" said a boy at the front of the classroom.

Tarah shook her head in frustration. Darcy knew Brisana was taking in every word, but she didn't care.

Just then, someone snickered, and Darcy noticed that everyone in the class had suddenly turned toward the front of the room. She looked up and saw a middle-aged white man in tan pants and a lab coat. He was sitting on top of the teacher's desk. Darcy had not even heard him enter the classroom.

"Are you two finished?" he asked. Someone giggled.

Overhead the bell signaling the start of class blared loudly, breaking the moment.

Darcy took a deep breath. She swallowed down her anger like a poison that left a bitter taste in her mouth.

"Yeah, we're done all right," she grumbled.

"Aww, c'mon, Darce," Tarah whispered, crossing her arms and slumping back in her chair. "Don't be that way."

Darcy could feel tears trying to gather in her eyes. But her resentment was stronger, holding the tears back, planting the hurt deep in her gut where it could

grow like a tumor.

As soon as class ended, Darcy stood up at her desk. She saw Tarah attempt to reach out to her and heard the beginning of an apology.

But it didn't matter.

Without a word, Darcy turned around, grabbed her things, and walked out, leaving her old friend behind.

Chapter 6

At lunchtime, Darcy looked for Hakeem but couldn't find him. She didn't know his schedule and wasn't about to ask Tarah for it. All she could do was wait until the end of the day. Then she'd tell him what was on her mind and end it once and for all.

In the cafeteria, she grabbed a soda and headed to an empty table. She wanted to be as far from Tarah as possible. Just thinking about how Tarah had hidden the truth from her made Darcy's stomach turn.

So what if Hakeem was her friend too.

So what if she knew Hakeem longer.

So what if she tried to get us to talk.

Tarah still should have told me everything, Darcy thought as she sipped her

soda and flipped through the few notes she managed to take in chemistry class.

"I told you, Darcy," said a voice, interrupting her. She looked up to see Brisana carrying a lunch tray. A thin smile stretched across her face.

"Don't start with me right now, Brisana," Darcy grumbled, closing her notebook. "I know you just want to rub it in."

"That's not true. Believe me, if I wanted to do that, you'd know it," Brisana said, sitting down across from her. "I just wanted to see how you're doing, that's all."

"How do you think I'm doing?" Darcy muttered. "My boyfriend, I mean *ex*-boyfriend, found someone else, and my best friend lied to hide it from me."

"You mean *ex*-best friend," Brisana said, eyeing Darcy carefully.

"Yeah, I guess so," Darcy replied with a shrug, her anger pushing the sadness away, but just barely.

"I don't mean to be rude, but what did you think was gonna happen?" Brisana said, sprinkling dressing on a small salad she got for lunch. "I mean, Hakeem's a guy. You two broke up. Did you think he was gonna stay single forever?"

60

"No, but—"

"And Tarah's always been closer to Cooper and Hakeem than to you. Now that Hakeem's living with her boyfriend, it's only gonna get worse."

"Yeah, but—"

"I mean I bet they all decided months ago to lie to you, the way *they* talk," Brisana said, rolling her eyes.

Darcy's blood was boiling. She hated to think of them all getting together and deciding to keep the secret from her, but it made sense.

That would explain the silences at Niko's. The strange glances. Darcy felt like her head was about to explode, like she was the plate Dad shattered into a thousand useless pieces.

"If you ask me," Brisana continued, slicing through a piece of lettuce, "I think you need to get real, Darcy. Those people are never gonna change. You need to move on. Not just from Hakeem, but from all of them."

Darcy tossed her notebook into her book bag. She didn't want to admit it, but for once she agreed with Brisana's advice. If Tarah, Cooper, and Hakeem had no trouble lying to her, what kind of friends were they? She imagined what

they must have said to each other before they went to Niko's.

"Don't worry, bro. I ain't gonna say nothin' to her," Cooper probably said. Darcy could almost see him slapping hands with Hakeem.

"She won't hear nothin' from me neither," Tarah would have replied.

Thinking about it made Darcy want to scream. And deep down beneath the white-hot anger that stormed in her chest, Darcy felt something else even stronger than rage. She felt pain.

It hurt that Hakeem had already replaced her. It hurt that their friends had helped hide his secret. Hurt that the trust she had put in them was broken, that the friendship she depended on each day was not what she thought it was.

You need to move on. Brisana's advice made sense.

"Maybe you're right," Darcy said, though she wished it weren't true. "I guess I was wrong about all of them."

"It's okay, Darce," Brisana replied with a grin that was somehow both warm and cold at the same time. *"I'm* still your friend."

Darcy's hands were shaking when

the final bell rang.

She rushed to her locker, grabbed her books and headed out the front doors of Bluford ready to confront Hakeem.

At the bottom of the steps, she joined a few other students leaning against a fence watching people exit the building. As Darcy waited, her heart racing, hundreds of kids slowly poured out of the school. Some got into cars, others hopped onto yellow buses lined outside, and many just walked home.

The first person Darcy recognized was her sister. Darcy hoped Jamee wouldn't see her, but their eyes met. Jamee headed straight to her with a wide smile on her face.

"Oh my God, Darce! I had the best day," Jamee gushed. "Me, Amberlynn, and Cindy are in the same English class with your old teacher, Mr. Mitchell. He's so cool. Then there's this guy, Tyray, who's already sweatin' Amberlynn. I think he's a jerk, but he's really cute," Jamee went on.

Darcy ignored her, watching as more people walked out of Bluford's main doors. Finally, she spotted Hakeem at the top of the steps. Tarah and Cooper were

right behind him. No one was smiling. They weren't even talking to each other.

Darcy's mouth suddenly went dry.

"Are you ready to go home?" Jamee asked. "Honestly, I don't even want to go back there. All day I kept trying to forget about what happened. I couldn't even sleep last night."

"Look, Jamee," Darcy said, trying to stay calm. She knew she should talk to her, but not now. Not with Hakeem getting closer. "Can we just talk about this later? Now isn't a good time. I'm waiting for someone."

"Well, excuse me!" Jamee said, taking a step back and looking a bit hurt. "Who are you waiting for?"

"Just go home, Jamee. I'll be there soon."

Darcy knew Cooper spotted her leaning against the fence. She saw him whisper something to Tarah, and all three of them stared and then looked away.

"Hey, here come your people, Darce," Jamee announced. "Why does everyone look so upset?"

Darcy didn't answer. Her eyes were focused on Hakeem, who stepped ahead of Cooper and slowly descended the steps. When he reached the bottom, he shook

his head and put his hands out as if he was surrendering. Now was the moment she'd waited for, the time to end it with all of them. Darcy took a deep breath.

But just as she was about to speak, someone stepped in front of her.

"*There* you are," said a voice Darcy had never heard before. "I've been waiting here for ten minutes. I was startin' to wonder if I was at the wrong Bluford."

Darcy watched as a beautiful light-skinned woman in a black tank-top rushed toward Hakeem. She had close-cropped hair and wore jeans that hung low on her curvy hips, leaving part of her flat stomach exposed. She was at least three inches taller than Darcy.

The girl walked right up and gave Hakeem a hug. His arms didn't move, and his eyes turned to Darcy even as the mysterious stranger clung to his neck.

Behind him, Cooper's and Tarah's eyes were wide open. Tarah's hands pressed against her cheeks as if she was watching a car accident happen right in front of her.

"No she didn't!" Cooper said, shaking his head. "Tell me I didn't just see that, Tar."

"Oh, she did it all right," Tarah

replied somberly. "Your eyes ain't lyin'."

"*Who's that*?" Jamee asked. "And what's she doing hugging Hakeem?"

Darcy knew who it was—the girl Brisana warned her about. Everything Brisana told her was true. And what Tarah said proved to be lies. Darcy knew what she had to do.

Without a word, she walked over to Hakeem.

"What are you d-d-doing here, Anika?" Hakeem said, shifting his eyes to her and then back to Darcy. He looked like he was about to be sick to his stomach.

"I thought I'd surprise you. I got off work early, and I didn't feel like sitting in my cousin's apartment, so I thought I'd—"

"Excuse me," Darcy interrupted, tapping Anika's shoulder and glaring at Hakeem. "You need to finish this conversation some other time because Hakeem and I need to talk. *Now*."

"Who you think you are talkin' to me that way?" Anika challenged, letting go of Hakeem and turning toward her. "You don't know me."

"Darcy, look, don't do this—"

"*You're* Darcy?" Anika asked, narrowing her eyes. "I know all about you. But

66

I can see he didn't tell you about me, did he?"

Darcy's jaw dropped at the sound of her name on Anika's lips.

"Anika, *don't!*" Hakeem barked.

"Don't what?" Anika said. "You mean you didn't tell her how we met in Detroit?"

"*Stop!*"

"How you kissed me the night you gave me my first guitar lesson—"

"*Anika!*"

"Or how we e-mailed each other all summer after I moved out here? Or how you wanted to see me as soon as you got back?"

"Girl, you better shut up 'cause you're lyin' like a snake," Tarah warned, stepping right up to Anika. "Don't listen to her, Darcy. She's just tryin' to cause trouble 'cause she knows you mean more to Hakeem than she does, and she can't stand it."

"Who are *you?*" Anika asked, glaring at Tarah.

"Never mind who I am. You better start thinkin' more about who *you* are. Around here, you don't just come up spreadin' lies and talkin' to my friend like that. You ain't got no right."

67

"Whatever," Anika said, stepping close to Hakeem. "I ain't scared. I've seen worse than you where I come from."

Darcy felt like she had been stabbed. Each detail pushed the knife deeper, cut into the final threads that held her to Hakeem, sliced so deeply that for a second Darcy couldn't even speak.

"My cousin was right about you," Hakeem yelled, turning away from Anika and walking over to Darcy. "He said you were crazy jealous."

"*Jealous*?" Anika repeated, crossing her arms and inspecting Darcy as if she was trying to check out the damage she caused. "I just wanted her to know the truth, that's all. I mean, she does deserve that, right? Besides, I ain't stupid. I know how girls are. And I don't want her getting all confused and thinking maybe there's still something between you two."

"Darcy, it isn't like the way she's s-saying." Hakeem began to explain. "I never—"

"I don't even care anymore," Darcy cut in, unable to listen to his excuses. "Hakeem, you should have just told me about her, not snuck around at the mall so I had to hear about it from someone

else. Just forget we ever had anything." Darcy turned away from him and glared at Tarah and Cooper. Anger burned like flames in her chest.

"Coop, I can almost understand where you're coming from with all this. You and Hakeem are like brothers, and you were just trying to protect him. But Tarah, what you did to me was so low I can't believe it. Don't ever call me your *girl* again, not after this. I never would've hid this from you, and I never would've thought you'd hide it from me," Darcy said, turning away from them both.

"You can keep him, Anika," Darcy continued, eyeing Hakeem for the last time. "I'm done. And if you want my advice, don't trust him or any of them."

"Darcy, c'mon, girl. You got us all wrong," Cooper protested.

Darcy ignored him. She turned and began walking home. Seconds later, she heard footsteps behind her and felt a hand on her shoulder, Hakeem's hand.

"Darcy, I'm sorry," he said.

"Don't talk to me."

"I didn't mean for things to happen this way."

"Yeah, well they did," she replied, shrugging off his hand. "I don't want to

69

talk to you again. I'm done."

Darcy wiped her eyes and walked faster, and Hakeem let her go. In just one afternoon, she'd lost her first real boyfriend and two of her closest friends. It hurt so much she couldn't even feel the pain, like a wound so deep all the nerves were destroyed.

Even the thought of Anika didn't sting as much as it did at first. In place of pain, a cold numbness was setting in, a feeling that something inside Darcy had finally died.

Chapter 7

Just keep walking.

Darcy repeated the words to herself as she rushed away from Bluford. She wished the school and all the people she knew there could just disappear, but there was no escape, not even at home. There she'd have to deal with her parents and the questions Jamee would ask her about what just happened. She felt trapped.

Without slowing down, Darcy walked right by her house and headed straight to the cemetery where her grandparents were buried. She needed to see Grandma.

Passing through the main gates, Darcy saw an old woman place a bundle of flowers in front of a weathered headstone. She watched as the woman spoke quietly to herself and raised a tissue to

her eyes. Darcy remembered a time years ago when she'd visited the cemetery with Grandma. They'd gone to put flowers at Darcy's grandfather's grave. He died of a heart attack when Darcy was five.

"*The Lord works in mysterious ways, Angelcake,*" Grandma told her then. "*Your grandfather's been gone six years already, rest his soul. There was a time I used to say I wouldn't want to live without him. But now I see if I weren't here, I'da missed being with you, Jamee, and your mother,*" Grandma confessed as she rested flowers on the ground.

Darcy remembered the day well because it was the only time she saw her grandmother cry.

"*As you get older, you start seein' that everything happens for a reason. Sometimes even the worst things turn out to be blessings in disguise. Heck, if we didn't have rain, we couldn't enjoy the sunshine, right Angelcake?*" Grandma had asked her. There was a smile on her face that was both sad and beautiful at the same time, a smile Darcy could still see when she closed her eyes.

On that day, Darcy wasn't in the mood to be happy. Dad's loss was still

fresh then, and it had felt like a death in the family. But Grandma's words made it a little easier, even if Darcy didn't fully believe or understand them.

If only Grandma was here now, Darcy thought as she approached the familiar granite headstone. Though it had been just a few months since Grandma passed away, the blanket of grass over her grave had already grown in so much that it nearly matched the surrounding ground. Another month, and it would blend in with the hundreds of other graves that stretched in quiet rows in the corner of the city.

Darcy sat down and ran her hand across the warm granite and traced her fingers along the words etched in the stone.

Annie Louella Duncan
Beloved
Wife   Mother   Grandmother

Birds chirped in trees overhead as Darcy began talking, telling Grandma about the trouble with her friends, the arguments with her parents, and her fears about the future.

"I just don't know what to do," she admitted, shaking her head as if

Grandma was sitting in front of her listening to every word like she used to. "It feels like everything is just falling apart, and I can't stop it. I miss you so much."

Darcy was crying softly when she suddenly heard footsteps. She quickly wiped her eyes and looked up to see Jamee. She must have followed her all the way from school. Their eyes met for a few seconds, and Darcy hoped her sister wouldn't say something stupid or expect her to talk about what happened. Jamee seemed to understand. Without a word, she sat down and put her arm on Darcy's shoulder.

The two were still for a long time before Darcy said what was on her mind, something the day's drama and the silence of Grandma's grave slowly taught her.

"We're not kids anymore," Darcy said.

Jamee nodded thoughtfully.

Maybe Jamee didn't fully understand. *Not yet*, Darcy thought. But they were the truest words Darcy could say about what had happened. Images of Mom yelling at Dad, the plate shattering on the floor, and Hakeem kissing Anika poured through her mind as she continued.

"Everything that happens from now on, *we* have to deal with it. Grandma's not here to take care of it for us. No one is," Darcy added.

"Don't forget about Mom and Dad," Jamee replied. "They're here for us . . . sort of."

Darcy glared at Jamee but didn't say anything. She knew in her mind that her parents were in trouble, that money problems and the stress of the new baby were taking a toll on them. But she didn't have the heart to tell Jamee what she was really thinking. That the days ahead were going to be difficult. That things would have to change in order for the family to survive. In the past, Grandma had stepped in and made the world right. But she was gone. Who would step up next?

Nearby a young couple placed a tiny American flag in front of a newly dug grave.

"Sometimes even the worst things turn out to be blessings in disguise."

Darcy heard Grandma's words echo in her mind, and she prayed they would be true. But as she looked to the future and thought of her friends and family, she couldn't see how.

Darcy took a deep breath as she got closer to the house. Jamee was right behind her. They had walked back from the cemetery together without a word. Darcy knew they were both wondering about the same thing.

Had Dad come home?

The house was silent when they entered. Darcy knew right away it was empty, though she could smell Dad's cologne in the air. He must have been there not long ago.

A note had been left on the kitchen counter. Spread across it were four $20 bills. Darcy pushed the money aside and picked up the note. Jamee came close to read it with her.

Mattie—I took the job at Empire Cabs. I'll be working days at the store and nights on the road. This is how we'll take care of things until I find something better. The money's yours—one night of tips. You CAN trust me.—Carl

"See, he didn't leave," Jamee said, a smile of relief on her face. "He's not going anywhere, Darce. He's just got a new job, that's all."

But Darcy's eyes were on something

else that troubled her more than any note. Next to the kitchen sink, sitting on the counter, was an empty brown beer bottle. Darcy picked it up and noticed it still contained a few drops of beer at the bottom. The sight made her head spin.

Just before Dad left years ago, he started drinking heavily. Darcy could remember the odor on his breath, the loud way he talked, the smelly beer bottles he started leaving around the house. When he first came back to the family, he told them how drinking helped him throw his life away. He'd said it again months ago when Darcy's Aunt Charlotte came over for dinner and offered him a glass of fancy wine.

"No thanks, Charlotte. I'm not touching that stuff again," he'd declared. *"Me and alcohol don't mix well."* Now he was going back on his word.

"It's not what you're thinking, Darcy," Jamee said quickly, though her face looked as if she'd seen a ghost. "I mean Dad wouldn't do that again."

"Well, what else could it be?" Darcy replied, throwing the bottle away.

"Maybe he had some friends over or something," Jamee suggested.

"Or maybe he's drinking again,"

Darcy cut back, wishing it weren't true.

Just then Darcy heard a car outside. She peered through a window to see her mother pulling up. Quickly Darcy folded up the note and put it back on the counter.

"We can't tell Mom about this," Jamee said, her eyes focused on the bottle. "She'll lose it again."

"Well, we can't just lie to her," Darcy insisted. "This is important, Jamee. She has a right to know."

Jamee looked out the window and rubbed her forehead as if she were in pain.

"Look, Darcy. Don't go crazy. This isn't new. I've found a few of them—"

"*What?!* And you never said anything?" Darcy yelled, unable to believe her ears. She remembered the bottle on the steps last night and Dad's late-night walks. He *had* been drinking again. Not only had her friends been keeping secrets, but her own sister had too. "How could you hide something like that from us after all he did?"

"I knew you'd flip out, that's why. You'd go crazy, and Mom would act like it's the end of the world and things would just get worse around here. Look,

it's not a big deal. It's just beer," Jamee replied, avoiding Darcy's stare.

"If it's not a big deal, you wouldn't be keeping it a secret from me or Mom," Darcy said.

Jamee hid the bottle deep in the trash can.

"You're trying to protect Dad, aren't you? You're always on his side."

"No, it's not that," Jamee paused, struggling for words. "I'm trying to protect *us*, Darcy. I just want things to be okay. No more screaming and yelling, you know? If Mom finds out about this, I'm scared what she'll do. I'm scared of what will happen."

Darcy knew Jamee meant what she said. But the idea of lying to her mother seemed so wrong. Outside, a heavy car door slammed. Mom would be walking through the door in seconds.

"I'm scared too, Jamee, but if you have to lie just to keep the peace, what's the point? I mean what kinda family are we if the only thing that holds us together is a lie?"

Jamee shook her head. "Please don't tell her, Darcy," she said, desperation in her voice, as if she was begging. "Don't do it. *Please*."

The front door opened then, and Darcy heard heavy footsteps moving closer.

"Girls? Carl? Anyone here?"

Darcy could hear the weariness in her mother's voice.

"We're in the kitchen, Mom," Darcy said.

Across from her, Jamee shook her head. "Don't do it," she whispered.

Darcy took a deep breath and tried to think of a gentle way to tell the truth just as her mother stepped into the kitchen.

"Did your father call?" Mom asked, walking slowly toward the counter. Darcy knew by the way she moved that her feet were sore and her back was aching. "Did either of you see him?"

Darcy looked at Jamee and then at Mom. For a second she couldn't speak as she stared at the dark circles beneath her mother's eyes and the wrinkles that stretched across her forehead. If it were possible, Darcy could swear Mom had aged five years since she saw her this morning.

"I didn't see him, but he left a note," Darcy answered finally. Jamee handed Mom the note along with the money.

Mom read it, took a deep breath and

sighed. For a second, she looked as if she was about to collapse with relief.

"Everything's okay, Mom," Jamee said. "He was just at work, that's all."

"He's a stubborn man, but I guess I can't fault him for trying to do the right thing," Mom said, rereading the note and putting the money in her pocket. "I don't want him driving a cab in the middle of the night, but I was wrong to come down so hard on him, and I was wrong to put you two in the middle of it. I'm sorry," she confessed, looking more exhausted than ever.

"And Jamee . . ." Without another word, Mom embraced Jamee and whispered something in her ear. The two hugged quietly, and then Mom reached an arm around Darcy. "What would I do without you two?" she sighed.

Darcy glanced at Jamee's tears and then at her mother's tired face. There was no way she could tell her about the beer bottle hidden nearby. Sure, it was a lie, and by keeping silent she was adding to it. But it seemed crueler to tell Mom the truth in such a state. Doing so would shatter her like a piece of glass.

But Dad's secret couldn't last forever. Her mind turned to her own friends and

how just hours ago the truth tore them all to pieces. Dad's problem would do the same thing to her family.

"Everything okay with you girls today?" Mom asked. "I got so caught up, I forgot to ask you about your first day of school."

"I had the greatest first day, Mom," Jamee said, explaining all the details Darcy had already heard.

Mom yawned and rubbed her temples when Jamee finished. She turned to Darcy then. "And what about you?" she said. "I bet it was great seeing Hakeem and the rest of the gang again."

Darcy couldn't raise her eyes or look at her mother's face. In her mind, she thought of the new baby resting in Mom's belly. She knew the truth would destroy everything. And a simple lie could give them all peace, at least for a little while.

"It was nice, Mom," Darcy said finally, deciding to keep the peace for another day. "Just like old times," she added, escaping down the dark hallway to her room alone.

Chapter 8

It was pitch-black when Darcy heard the sounds. First a thud of footsteps as someone walked into the kitchen. Then the "thunk" of the heavy refrigerator door followed by the quick hiss and snap of a beer bottle opening.

It was Dad. He must have just come home from a night of work. Darcy crept out of her bed and into the hallway. She wasn't going to let him drink again.

As she reached the kitchen, she noticed it was empty and dark. Confused, she took a step forward and felt a stinging pain in her foot. She reached down and felt something sharp sticking from her heel. She could feel wetness on her fingers too. Something warm was dripping off her foot.

Blood.

In a panic, she hopped to the bathroom to grab a towel, but when she got there, the bathroom counter was empty except for a single beer bottle glistening in the dark. Darcy turned on the light and noticed her foot then. A shard of broken china stabbed deep into her heel. The gash it opened was as long as her thumb.

"Mom! Dad! I cut myself bad, and I'm bleeding," she cried.

No one answered. They must be asleep, she thought.

"Mom! Dad! Jamee?!" Darcy yelled out again. Her blood was spilling onto the floor in thick red drops.

In the mirror, Darcy saw her reflection. A frightened girl holding her bloody foot stared back at her. She looked desperate. Alone. Almost childlike. But then Darcy saw other faces in the mirror.

Anika's angry glare.

Cooper, Tarah, and Hakeem laughing at her.

Her parents in tears yelling at her.

And Brian Mason. He seemed to reach at her from the mirror, his hand piercing through it as if it were water.

"No!" she screamed.

The mirror exploded into a shower of glass that rained down in jagged pieces

falling toward her face.

"No!"

Darcy bolted upright in her bed, covered in a layer of sweat, her heart pounding like a drum. She reached down to her foot. Her heel was fine. No blood. No broken plate. Darcy sighed and looked at her clock. It was 5:17 in the morning.

She laid back and looked at the ceiling, dreading the day ahead.

"What am I gonna do?" she whispered into the dark.

In her mind, she kept seeing herself in the mirror. A scared, lonely girl. It may have been a dream, but she knew part of it was real. The events of the past days had left her more alone than ever. Cut off from her family. Her ex-boyfriend. Even her best friend.

"You don't just drop your people," Tarah had said. *"When stuff happens, which it always does, you work through it . . . it's what you gotta do when somethin's important."*

Darcy felt as if she was the one who'd been dropped. Everyone had let her down somehow, walked away from her, lied to her. Betrayed her.

But alone in the darkness of her quiet

bedroom, part of her knew it wasn't that simple. She had cut off Tarah, not the other way around. And she had done other things too. Kept her secrets about Brian hidden from Hakeem, lied to Mom about her first day at school, hid the news about the beer bottle from her.

That's different, she thought to herself.

Sure, she'd lied. But she did it to keep the peace. To keep everyone happy. To keep things from flying apart like the mirror in her dream. Telling the truth would have shattered everything. Darcy had lied for the right reasons.

But what if Tarah felt the same way? What if she lied for the same reasons? The questions made Darcy's head spin. She flipped onto her side, unable to get comfortable.

"We're not kids anymore," she whispered to herself. The words she'd spoken at Grandma's grave seemed truer than ever. When Darcy was younger, the world was simpler and easier somehow. Things were either right or wrong. Good or bad.

But now everything was mixed and messy, full of cracks and broken pieces like the mirror in her dreams.

Darcy sat up in her bed, giving up on

sleep. She couldn't stop her mind from racing through everything that had happened. Her thoughts still went back to Tarah, the person whose actions hurt her most.

"*You don't lie to your friends,*" Darcy wanted to say. "*I trusted you.*"

"*You don't drop your friends,*" would be Tarah's reply. "*I'm one of them.*"

It was a voice Darcy couldn't completely ignore, even though she wanted to. Tired and frustrated, she stretched and dragged herself out of bed.

Outside, the dark was giving way to the coming dawn, and Darcy could see the dim outlines of pictures she'd hung on the wall opposite her bed. There were two old photos of Hakeem, a picture of Cooper and Tarah, and a snapshot of all four of them at the beach.

She hadn't taken them down.

Not yet.

Two hours later, Darcy headed out the front door with Jamee. Unlike yesterday, she hoped her sister would walk to Bluford without her, but Jamee didn't cooperate. Instead, she'd waited while Darcy packed her bookbag, and then she rushed out the door the instant

Darcy decided to leave.

Darcy was not in the mood for her or Bluford as they turned up the block toward the high school. Just a few doors from their house, Darcy spotted a brown beer bottle. The sight of it left a queasy feeling in the pit of her stomach. They still had to deal with Dad.

"Me and Dez got in a fight last night on the phone," Jamee said, glancing quickly at the bottle and then at Darcy. "It was about you."

"*Me?*" Darcy replied. The last thing she wanted to think about was Jamee and her boyfriend, Cooper's little brother, arguing about her. "Don't you two have something better to talk about?"

"I'm serious, Darce. He told me Coop and Tarah are really upset about what happened yesterday. I said it serves them right, they should be upset for what they did. But he got mad at me, sayin' we were both overreacting," Jamee explained.

"First of all, it's none of *his* business—or yours. You shouldn't have been there, Jamee. And second, I don't need any fourteen-year-old telling me what to do, especially not Coop's brother. What does he know anyway?" Darcy snapped.

"That's what *I* said. Now that we're at Bluford, he's been actin' all weird. I got so mad at him last night, we practically broke up," Jamee said as they crossed a street together. "I know it's not any of my business, but I just gotta say I think you were right about what you told everybody yesterday. If I were you, I'da lost it and started hitting somebody. Especially that girl huggin' Hakeem."

Darcy winced at her sister's words. Even though she meant well, Jamee was practically rubbing in what had happened.

"Thanks," Darcy said, hoping Jamee would drop the subject and talk about something else.

"Cindy and Amberlynn totally agree . . . I mean, about my fight with Dez," Jamee said quickly, her eyes suddenly darting away.

Darcy could a feel a headache building behind her eyes. Even though Jamee didn't exactly admit it, Darcy knew she'd told her friends everything about Hakeem. The private details of her relationship were now freshman gossip. People she didn't even know were already talking about how some strange girl from Detroit had ripped her

boyfriend away. Darcy was about to scream at Jamee when something caught her eye, a sight that made her heart jump into her throat.

A red Toyota with oversized tires and chrome rims waited at a traffic light. It sat low on its wide wheels, just inches from the ground. It was a car Darcy knew well, one she'd even gone to the beach in months ago when Hakeem left.

No.

It can't be.

He's supposed to be gone, hundreds of miles away. That's what his sister told her after the attack. But the Toyota up the street looked every bit like Brian Mason's.

Darcy stood frozen on the sidewalk, watching the car turn a corner and disappear. Her mouth was suddenly dry, and she could hear ringing in her ears. A tremor raced down her back.

Relax, she thought, trying to stay calm. *Be realistic. Maybe he sold his car. Maybe someone else tricked out a Toyota so it looked exactly like his. There could be hundreds of cars just like it on the road,* Darcy tried to convince herself.

"Are you okay?" Jamee asked, breaking Darcy's thoughts. "You look like you

saw a ghost or something."

Darcy took a deep breath and tried to hide that her hands were cold and trembling. At least Jamee hadn't seen the car and figured out what it meant. At least that story would not be part of Bluford's gossip. Not yet anyway.

"I'm fine," Darcy said, forcing herself to walk forward. "I don't want you or your friends talking about me or Hakeem anymore, okay?"

"Yeah, whatever," Jamee said, eying Darcy carefully. "What is it? Why are you so upset all the sudden?"

Darcy knew Jamee sensed something was wrong, but she wasn't about to tell her the truth.

"I told you, *I'm fine*," Darcy repeated, stepping ahead of her sister.

But as they approached the lot outside of Bluford, Darcy was sure her biggest secret had come back to haunt her.

Brian Mason had returned.

Darcy still felt lightheaded at lunchtime. But she forced herself to focus on her morning classes.

Chemistry had been the most difficult with Tarah nearby. The two didn't say a word the entire period, though at

several points Darcy wanted to turn around and talk to her. She could almost sense that Tarah felt the same way, though neither could find the words. Darcy wasn't even sure what they were anymore.

As Tarah walked out of class, she dropped a folded piece of paper on Darcy's desk. Darcy recognized Hakeem's scratchy handwriting immediately. She read the note once in class and then again while she waited for Brisana at their lunch table.

Dear Darcy,

I am SO sorry about yesterday. I'm even more sorry for never telling you about Anika. I was afraid if you learned the truth, you'd be hurt. But now I've hurt you more.

You deserve the truth, so here it is. I was so depressed in Detroit without you. Anika was my neighbor. I met her one night when I was playing my guitar. We liked each other right away. We hung out a few times, and we kissed. But that's ALL that happened. I swear.

The girl has problems. She ended up leaving Detroit, and I thought that was

the last I'd see her. Then she wrote
and told me she was living with her
cousin an hour from here. I'm being
straight up, Darcy. We e-mailed each
other all summer. I promised I'd meet
her if I ever got back. That's what
happened on Saturday. I had no idea
she was going to show up yesterday.

I should've told you all this sooner,
but I was scared. And to be honest, I'm
confused. The reason I started seeing
Anika was because we were apart. I
never thought I'd see you again, but
here I am. Yesterday reminded me of
how much we had. It seems wrong to
let it all go. But I understand if that's
what you want.

No matter what, I'm sorry. Maybe we
can go to Niko's again, just you and
me? Let me know.

She stares at me, her eyes onyx fire.
I burn in them. I've been a liar.
What I did was a dumb mistake.
What we had shouldn't break.
If I could do it over again,
I'd fix it all. There'd be no end.

Love, Hak

"What's that?" Brisana asked, sitting down at the table with her usual salad. Her eyes were focused on the paper in Darcy's shaking hands.

"It's a note from Hakeem," Darcy admitted, slipping it into her notebook.

"What's *he* want?"

"I'm not sure. Maybe a second chance," Darcy replied, her head spinning with the news and the answer she knew she had to give him.

"*Please!* Don't tell me you're going to take him back, not after what he did with that girl," Brisana said. She looked as if she had just tasted something sour in her salad.

Darcy didn't say a word. Instead, she grabbed a piece of paper and wrote a short reply back to Hakeem. She dropped it on Tarah's table without a word just before the lunch period ended. She knew it would get to Hakeem right away.

She'd written just four words to him.

"Meet me after school."

Chapter 9

Hakeem was already outside when Darcy headed out of Bluford. She saw him pacing at the bottom of the steps where she had been the day before.

What a difference a day makes, Darcy thought to herself as she approached. She was still angry at him, but she had to put an end to the lies. He'd dumped his secrets, but hers were still gnawing at her.

She'd given up on getting back together with him. But she knew she'd never be able to clear her head unless she told him what really happened. Only then would she free herself from the guilt about lying to him. Only then could she look at him and know she'd done the right thing. With him or without him, it was the only way she could move on.

And it had to happen now.

"Hi, Darcy," Hakeem said, his voice wavering slightly. She could tell he was fighting his stutter.

"Let's go to the park," she said, avoiding his nervous gaze. "There's something I need to tell you."

He nodded, and they walked several blocks without a word. In her mind, Darcy tried to rehearse what she'd say, but everything was jumbled. They crossed into the park where they once walked hand-in-hand. Only now they kept their distance, careful not to touch. She led him to a bench and sat down.

"Darcy, I just want to say this one more time. I'm sorry—"

"I don't want you to say anything else until you hear what I've got to tell you," she said, cutting him off. Each of his apologies added to the guilt pressing down on her. She needed him to stop until he'd heard everything. Then he'd have a choice to make. So would she.

"If he's the person I think he is, he'll handle it just right," Tarah had said. *"If not, you're better off without him."* Now was the time to find out.

"What is it, Darcy?" he asked.

"When you were away, I started seeing

someone too," she said.

Hakeem's brown eyes opened wide. *"What?"*

Without pausing, Darcy told him how she'd met Brian, how he'd comforted her when Hakeem left. She even mentioned their walks on the beach and how she'd kissed him. But she held back the rest of the truth, the part about the attack. It was her darkest secret, a knot of shame and hurt she still wasn't sure she could tell.

Hakeem's face looked pained, as if he was squinting at the sun or something, but his eyes were aimed down at the ground.

"Why didn't you tell me about him? You should have told me, Darcy," he said, kicking his heels against the edge of their bench.

"And you should have told me about Anika before I saw her hugging you," Darcy cut back.

Hakeem shook his head. Darcy knew what he was feeling. Hurt and jealousy, the sour mix that made her want to scream yesterday.

"I'm not gonna lie, Darcy. I don't like thinking about you with someone else. It hurts me right here," he said, slapping

his chest. "But what can I say? We broke up. I couldn't expect you to just stop living after I left. What kinda person would I be if I did that?"

Hakeem stared at her then. His eyes seemed to gaze right into her, and Darcy had to look away. He was showing himself to be what she remembered, what led her to him in the first place. He was smart, kind, friendly, and deep. He was trying his best to be straight up with her. She knew how hard that was. She still hadn't managed to be straight up with him. The secrets she'd hidden for so long were falling away, but the biggest one still remained.

Darcy turned back and noticed the park was completely empty. Everything seemed still and tense. Even the birds grew quiet, and the sun hung like a giant red eye staring down at them. She braced herself for what she had to say next, the secret that hurt her the most and haunted her even this morning as she watched the Toyota pull up the street.

"There's something else, Hakeem. Something I always wanted to hide from you, but I can't anymore," she said.

Hakeem massaged his forehead and

temples like he had a headache, but then he shook off whatever pained him, sat upright, took a deep breath, and focused on her. "You can tell me anything, Darcy."

"Something happened with Brian," she admitted, struggling for the words she knew she had to say. "I mean nothing *really* happened, but it almost did. My father stopped everything, but before that Brian almost . . . I mean things just got—"

"What is it, Darcy? What are you trying to say?"

"We were kissing on his couch. I shouldn't have even been there. I was so stupid, but he seemed so nice, and I was missing you," Darcy explained, unable to look in Hakeem's eyes.

"What happened? What did he do?" Hakeem asked, his voice rising with concern and anger.

"He wouldn't stop," Darcy answered. Her words seemed to freeze the entire park. For several seconds, nothing moved. Not the ants on the ground. Not the leaves in the trees. Not even cars on the street nearby.

"*What?!*"

Darcy couldn't raise her head to look

at Hakeem, but she couldn't hold back the truth either. "I asked him to stop, but he just kept pushing me, you know? I got so scared. If my dad hadn't come over, I don't know what would have happened," she explained. She even told him about the nightmares, how Tarah helped her, and the scare she had on the way to Bluford.

That's when she realized Hakeem wasn't okay. He was sitting with his arms crossed and his legs twitching with nervous energy. His face was bunched up in an angry scowl.

"Tarah knew about this and didn't tell me?" he asked, not waiting for an answer. "I can't believe it. Y'all are supposed to be my friends. If something serious happens, I should know about it," he protested.

"It wasn't her secret to tell. It was mine, and I would have never forgiven her if she told you. She was just protecting me, that's all."

"*Protecting you?!* It don't seem like anyone's been doing that since I left. Where is this punk? Dude needs to learn a lesson," Hakeem yelled.

"No, Hakeem. This was months ago. It's over—"

"It's *not* over, Darcy! You can't just drop this on me and expect me to be cool with it," Hakeem cut back. He stood up from the bench and started pacing in front of her like a caged lion. "That punk coulda hurt you."

"Calm down!" Darcy said, moving into his path and putting her hands on his chest. "I'm okay. Nothing really happened."

"No, something *did* happen. I can't believe this is the first time I'm hearing about it. It's been months! Someone should have told me."

Darcy knew the feeling well. His words were the same as hers yesterday. And her reasons for hiding the truth weren't much different from his.

"I was scared of what you'd think about me," Darcy admitted. "Like maybe you'd blame me for what happened." She'd heard guys talk. She knew the ugly words they had for girls, especially one who went to a guy's apartment alone. Darcy hated the words and knew they were wrong, but Hakeem might not. She always feared he'd think less of her for what happened.

"*Blame you*? You didn't do this. The sorry coward who pushed you around is

the one I blame. I need to talk to him," Hakeem fumed, his eyes flashing with anger. He suddenly looked scary, his face hard and mean.

Darcy stepped back. She wasn't sure what to say to calm him down. She'd only wanted him to understand what happened. She hadn't expected him to flip out.

"There's nothing you need to say to him. It's done," Darcy replied.

"Coop know about this too?" he asked, ignoring her comment.

Darcy wasn't sure of the answer. Tarah was the only one who knew and could have told Cooper. But the more Darcy learned, the more she thought Tarah had kept her secret.

"It ain't right for me to be tellin' everybody's secrets, especially when the secrets can hurt people," Tarah had said. Darcy believed her.

"I don't think so," she answered. "Why?"

Hakeem turned away from her suddenly. "Look, Darcy. I gotta go. I'll call you later."

"Where are you going?" she called. She didn't like the stormy look on his face, the tightness in his jaw. "Hakeem?"

He didn't look back or slow down. Instead, he headed out of the park and back into the streets.

"Everything'll be all right," he called out as he left. "I just need to take a walk, that's all. I'll call you."

As she watched him walk away, Darcy wasn't sure exactly where Hakeem was going. But inside she knew what he was going to find once he got there—trouble.

Darcy rushed home unsure what to do.

Her mother was walking out the door when Darcy turned the corner onto their street. Mom was wearing her hospital ID badge as she slowly made her way to the car.

Darcy could see her mother was exhausted. But as she got closer, Darcy thought Mom looked even worse. Her face was gray and puffy. She almost looked sick, like she was fighting the flu or something.

"Where you going, Mom? Aren't you supposed to be taking nights off from now on?" Darcy asked.

Mom sat down slowly in the car as if her back was sore.

"Don't start lecturing me. I got enough of that from your sister. I don't need it from you too," Mom snapped. "Someone called out at the hospital, so I'm gonna fill in. They're gonna pay me overtime, and Lord knows we need the money if we're ever gonna afford this baby."

"Can't you let someone else go in?" Darcy asked. "You can't work like this. You're too tired."

Jamee walked outside. She must have heard them talking.

"That's enough from both of you. I'm going to work, and that's it. Even with his new job, your father's gonna have to work eighty hours a week to keep us above water once the baby's born. The more we can save up before then, the better. Now I'm sorry. You might not like it, but that's the way it's gonna have to be," Mom explained.

But Mom, Darcy wanted to say, *Dad's drinking again and you're the only one who doesn't see it. He's not going to be able to hold up under all that pressure.* Yet Darcy couldn't say a word even as she checked for beer bottles on the front step. There were none.

"Now I'll be back late, so don't wait up

for me. Your father said he was getting off early tonight. He should be back around ten. There's leftovers in the fridge," she explained, putting the car into gear.

"We're gonna have to tell her the truth, Jamee," Darcy said as soon as their mother pulled away. "We can't keep lying to her."

Jamee nodded somberly. "I found where he's hiding the beer. There's a cooler hidden in the crawl space under the house. I found a bottle cap in the backyard and saw this little panel that he pried open. I couldn't believe it."

Neither could Darcy until Jamee led her to a spot in their tiny backyard. Just as Jamee described, there was a thin metal panel right above the ground. Jamee pulled it away to reveal a blue cooler not much bigger than Darcy's bookbag. Inside were four bottles exactly like the empty one she'd found in the kitchen. Darcy shook her head in shock. Her father had been hiding his problem right underneath them.

"Maybe that's why he wanted this house," Jamee said bitterly. "Because he knew it had a hiding spot." Her voice was heavy with sadness, as if the image

she had of her father had been shattered forever.

"We have to tell Mom about this tonight, Jamee," Darcy said, putting the panel back in place. She wanted her mother to see it for herself. "As soon as she gets home."

A tear rolled down Jamee's face. "I'm scared of what's gonna happen."

"Me too," Darcy said, giving her a hug. "Me too."

A few hours later, Darcy's cell phone rang. Her heart jumped in her chest.

The moment she'd watched Hakeem storm out of the park, she felt something bad would happen. She was so sure she'd even tried to call Tarah and Cooper, but neither was home. She even thought about calling the police but then talked herself out of it.

What if you're wrong? What if he just needed to clear his head? She thought.

One thing that made her feel better was that no one had called her with bad news. Everything had been quiet. Until now.

She looked at the phone and saw that the call was from Tarah's house.

"Hello?"

"Hey girl. It's me," Tarah said. Darcy could hear the worry in her voice. "Look, I know we got lots to talk about, but somethin' serious is happenin', and I'm scared."

"What is it, Tarah?" Darcy asked, even though she already knew the answer.

"It's Coop and Hakeem. They're goin' after Brian. We gotta stop 'em before they do somethin' stupid."

Chapter 10

Darcy ran out of her house onto the dark street.

"Where you goin'? It's gettin' late," Jamee asked.

"Don't worry about it. I'll be back soon," Darcy yelled as she headed down the block. She knew she had to move quick. Tarah told her that Cooper and Hakeem left ten minutes ago. That meant they'd be at Brian's any second if they weren't there already.

"I ain't never seen Hakeem so upset," Tarah had explained. "He got all in my face for not tellin' him what happened to you. Coop tried to calm him down and that's when Hakeem told *him* what Brian did. Next thing I know, they're both racin' off in Coop's truck. You gotta do something, Darce. You're the only one

who can stop this now."

Darcy didn't know what she'd do as she raced to the corner and sprinted toward Brian's apartment building four blocks away. Tarah's house was on the other side of the neighborhood, a ten-minute drive. There was no time for her to get involved, Darcy knew that. She had to handle this on her own.

People on the sidewalk glared at her as she darted between them and plowed ahead. On one corner, a car skidded loudly as she dashed into the street. On another block, someone shouted a curse at her, but she didn't care. Her friends' lives were at stake.

A police car rolled by up ahead. Darcy was about to flag it down, but it sped off before she had a chance. She was only two blocks away.

Even at that distance, she could see the cement walls of the apartment building up ahead. Her eyes scanned up to the fourth floor window of the Masons' apartment. The lights were on.

The sight made her stomach tighten up like a fist. She could picture the inside of the apartment. The family pictures on the wall. The glass coffee table. The sofa where Brian pinned her.

The memory still filled her with an anger no words could describe. An anger that didn't fade as the weeks and months passed. An anger at guys who hurt others, who ignore it when a girl says *no*.

"Yo, take it easy. I don't see no fire," a man shouted as Darcy raced down the last block. She'd nearly hit him as she flew by.

Darcy heard someone yelling as she reached the parking lot next to the building. She turned and spotted Cooper's old pick-up truck. Its doors were open, its engine idling loudly. Next to it was a red Toyota.

This time Darcy was sure it was Brian's car.

In the beam of the truck's headlights, she saw Brian. He was wearing a loose black T-shirt and baggy jeans. A grease stain was on his pants as if he had been working on his car. Hakeem was in front of him, his face inches from Brian's. Cooper was right beside him.

"You think you're a man?" Hakeem growled. "I'm about to teach you what a man is right now."

"No!" Darcy yelled from across the lot, but no one seemed to hear her voice.

Hakeem lunged at Brian, sending two quick punches to his face, one to his chin, the other to his cheek. Darcy could hear the heavy blows landing as she rushed closer.

"No!" she screamed again, but the fight possessed them. She watched as Brian shoved Hakeem back and punched the side of his face, his knuckles hitting with a loud crack. She'd crossed the parking lot, stopping just a few feet away.

Cooper circled close like a shark ready to strike. Brian, struggling against Hakeem, was defenseless against him. Cooper's punches would not be blocked.

But Darcy didn't want it. She never asked for her friends to do this. She never wanted to see them risk their lives and futures for her, or waste them on a piece of trash like Brian.

"*Stop it!*" she ordered. Her voice couldn't be louder, but the boys struggled, cursing and punching like animals. Drops of blood stained Hakeem's shirt. Cooper's fists were raised like two hammers ready to destroy Brian.

Darcy knew she had to act.

"I said *stop it!*" she yelled, stepping right in front of Cooper. His eyes

widened at the sight of her, as if she had suddenly broken the spell he'd been under. He lowered his fists and backed up. "Help me break this up, Coop," she ordered.

Cooper shook his head like she'd asked him to do something impossible. Darcy cursed and rushed to Hakeem, pushing against him with all her might, trying to separate him from Brian. "Don't do this. He's not worth it," she screamed.

"Watch out!"

Darcy heard Cooper's warning, but her back was to Brian. She had just enough time to brace herself.

Whap!

She felt as if a bullet ripped into her back, though there was no gunshot. She knew it was Brian's fist that struck her from behind. The blow made her legs buckle but not fall.

She heard Cooper yelling something, but she focused on Hakeem, blocking out the pain. She stared into his eyes with something she hadn't felt in months. She wanted to stop him, to calm him, to protect him.

"Look at me!" she commanded, putting her hands on his face. "*Look at me!*"

Finally she saw the anger in his eyes begin to melt. Saw that he recognized her. She latched onto his shoulders even as he tried to shrug her off.

"What are you doin' here, Darcy?" he asked. "This ain't the place for you."

"It's not the place for you either. He's not worth it," she said.

"I ain't scared of either of you," Brian growled behind her. "Y'all just a couple of little boys."

Darcy turned to see Cooper and Brian circling each other. Cooper had shoved Brian back, kept him away from Darcy and Hakeem. He was protecting them, though he looked like he wanted to do more. She knew Hakeem wanted to too, but she got their attention. She forced them to pause. To think.

"And you're nothing but a coward who pushes girls around," she snapped back, walking over to him. It was the first time she faced him since the attack. But after the counseling and the fight, he seemed smaller somehow. Nothing like the Brian in her dreams.

"What you did to me was wrong, and you know it. Part of me wants to see you hurt, but then I'd be just like you. Now if you were really a man, you'd step up,

apologize and learn how to treat people. But I'm not holding my breath for that," she said, turning to Hakeem and Cooper. "My friends may be younger, but they're more man than you'll ever be."

Brian rolled his eyes, but Darcy didn't care. She was done with him. The nightmare of the beginning of the summer was over. She'd stood up to the monster and stared it down. But there were bigger monsters at home. She looked at her watch and realized Dad would be home in less than an hour.

"You are either crazy or the bravest girl I know," Cooper said as they walked away together back to his truck. "I ain't sure which yet."

"She's both," Hakeem said, putting his arm on Darcy's shoulder and turning to her. They stopped walking. "I'm sorry I wasn't here to protect you. I'm so sorry," he said, his voice wavering. He hugged her then, the truest embrace he'd ever given. For the first time since he'd been back, she felt glimmers of the past, a feeling of connection, of understanding, of honesty.

"I don't need you to protect me," she replied.

"She's right," Cooper chimed in from

his truck. "Maybe we need her to protect us. I can't wait to tell Tarah about all this."

"I got a few things I need to tell her too, Coop," Darcy said. She knew now that Tarah had been loyal to her all along, that she'd been in an impossible situation and did the best she could. It was all Darcy could ask of anyone. When she got a chance, she'd apologize. But not tonight.

Not with what waited in store for her.

Jamee was on the phone when Darcy walked in.

"*He's not there?*" she said into the phone. "Well, where is he? I was told he was getting off around ten." Jamee's eyes suddenly grew wide. She hung up the phone without saying goodbye.

"What is it? What's wrong?" Darcy asked.

"I'm trying to find Dad. The cab company said he had off today. But Mom said he was working tonight."

"Huh?"

"Don't you get it, Darcy? He lied to Mom. He's probably off drinking somewhere," Jamee said, sitting down on the couch and putting her face in her

115

hands. "After you left, Mom called. She hurt her back at work and needs a ride home. She didn't have Dad's new work number, so she asked me to call him. But he's not there. I don't know what to do. Everything's falling apart." Jamee's last words broke into gentle sobs.

Darcy looked at the clock. It was almost ten. She was about to call Cooper to ask for a ride when she heard a car pull up. She peeked out the window and saw Dad.

"He's here," Darcy said, feeling her hands tremble with nervous energy.

"If he's drunk, Darcy, I swear to God I will lose it," Jamee said.

Dad walked in a second later. Darcy and Jamee watched in icy silence as he took off his jacket. There was nothing unusual about the way he moved. If he drank anything, it wasn't much, Darcy thought.

"What's wrong with you two?" he asked as soon as he came into the living room. His eyes were on Jamee. It was clear she'd been crying.

"Mom called," Darcy said, "She hurt her back and needs a ride home. *Now.*"

"What happened?" Dad asked, his eyes widened with alarm. "Is she okay?"

"What do you care?" Jamee snapped. "If you were so concerned, you wouldn't have lied about where you were tonight."

Darcy watched as her father nodded and took a long, sad breath.

"Let's go get your mother. We'll talk when we know she's okay. I have a lot to tell you." He grabbed the keys he'd just put down and headed out the door.

Jamee flashed Darcy a look. She was giving up on Dad with every second, and it was tearing her apart inside. Darcy could read it on her sister's face.

Darcy felt it too. Their family was a ship that was slowly sinking under the sea.

Dad raced to the hospital. No one talked during the car ride, but they rushed out together and headed straight to the emergency room where Mom worked. Inside, the air smelled of floor cleanser and body odor.

In the hallway outside the ER, an entire family sat looking pale with worry. Inside, Darcy nearly collided with a middle-aged woman standing beside an old man in a wheelchair. He coughed loudly as Darcy passed. A horrible gurgling sound came from his lungs.

How can Mom spend so much time here? Darcy wondered.

Dad spoke to a doctor and was directed to a small office area just around the corner from the emergency room. Mom was there stretched out on a portable hospital bed. She looked like a patient, not a nurse.

"What happened, Mattie?" Dad asked, rushing to her side.

"I can't do it no more, Carl. My back gave out," Mom said. Darcy could see she had been crying too. Her eyes still glistened with tears. "Doctor tells me I gotta slow down or I'm gonna hurt myself and the baby."

"Then you better listen," Dad said. "That's what we've been telling you."

"But you're gonna have to work two jobs to make up for my lost overtime. Don't lie to me, Carl. You can't work that much. No one can," Mom said shaking her head sadly.

"We'll figure it out, Mattie," Dad said, glancing back at Darcy and Jamee. "You just have to have faith. I'm leaning on that a lot these days."

Jamee wept softly and leaned into Darcy. The ship was still sinking. Darcy could feel it slide, and she couldn't

stand it. There had to be something more she could do than just watch it happen.

"You can lean on me too," Darcy said suddenly.

"Huh?" Everyone turned to her.

"I've been thinking about it for a long time, and I've decided to work more. I know I can work twenty-five hours a week and still keep up my grades—"

"No, I won't let you do that," Mom said.

"It's what I'm gonna do, Mom," Darcy replied. It was true. She wouldn't take no for an answer.

"But—"

"Listen, Mom. I'm older now, and this is what I want to do. If my grades slip, I'll cut back. But if not, why shouldn't I work?"

"No, it's not right. We don't want to be a burden to you—"

"But we're family, Mom. That's what we do for each other. You and Grandma taught us that. Besides, I am that baby's big sister," Darcy added. "It's time for you to let me be that."

"I can help too. I can babysit for extra money," Jamee offered then. "I know it's not much, but it's something. I'm going

to be a big sister too."

Mom shook her head at her two daughters. "When did you two get so stubborn?" she asked.

"They take after you," Dad said, gently rubbing Mom's shoulder. He leaned back and looked at the girls, his own eyes glistening with tears of pride. "You and your mother."

At home, Mom went to her room immediately, and Dad sat up with the girls in the living room.

"I'm going to treat you like adults because you acted like adults tonight," Dad announced. "You can tell your mother now or later. I haven't told her because I didn't want to upset her with the baby, but I'll let you decide after you hear everything."

Darcy was hanging on his every word. She knew what was at stake. Would they survive as a family or not? Dad took a deep breath.

"You're right, Jamee. I wasn't at work tonight. I was at a meeting for people like me. People with drinking problems. It's called Alcoholics Anonymous. I used to go to these meetings all the time, but I got better and stopped going. With all

the stress, I started drinking again. Nothing serious, but I realized it could become a problem, so I got help. This week, I started going to the meetings every day. Being a cabby allows me to do that," he admitted.

"See this?" he said, holding up a small coin with a prayer on it. "This is a token I have to keep me from drinking. Your words tonight, your faces right now, that baby on the way. I've got plenty of reasons not to drink, and I swear I will work every day to make sure I don't. You girls, your mom, this family, are the most precious things in the world to me. I will not throw that away again. *Never*," Dad promised.

Darcy wiped her eyes as her father finished speaking. His words were pure and true, and she could see he believed them with all his heart. Jamee wrapped her arms around him, and Darcy embraced them both. They barely even noticed Mom standing at the edge of the living room listening to every word. She quietly joined them in the embrace, their tears flowing together.

They were still a family. A stronger family than Darcy realized.

"*Sometimes even the worst things*

turn out to be blessings in disguise."
Grandma's words seemed truer now than ever. At several points over the past few days, Darcy was sure her family and friendships were coming to an end, and her world would be forever broken. Now Darcy realized she had been wrong. Many things had changed, but nothing was destroyed.

Mom's tiredness forced her to get the rest she and the baby needed. Dad's problem actually brought him closer to the family, showed everyone the love and commitment he had made to them. And the stress of the past few days had also changed Darcy.

She was different than she'd been just a week ago. Older somehow. Wiser. Less scared. It was true she was not a child anymore. The events of the past week and the afternoon at Grandma's grave taught her that. But in place of the child she had been was something greater. Something more powerful.

A budding adult. A young woman.

Sure, she would now have to work harder, take more responsibility, help out her family more. Darcy knew that. But she also knew she joined a line of powerful women who had done that

before her. Her mother and her grandmother.

Now it was Darcy's turn. She felt honored to be in such company.

At 6:30 a.m., Darcy was awakened by a strange sound. A scratching noise. It was coming from the backyard. She bolted upright in her bed.

Please God. Don't let it be what I think it is.

Darcy ran to the window and looked out. Standing there alone in the yellow dawn was her father. He was pulling beer bottles from the crawl space, opening them, and pouring them gently into the grass.

Thank you, God.

She heard him tossing the bottles one-by-one into a trash can. Heard them shatter. A sound sweeter than any music.